Careers in Focus

Nursing

Ferguson Publishing Company
Chicago, Illinois

Andrew Morkes, *Managing Editor-Career Publications*
Carol Yehling, *Senior Editor*
Anne Paterson, *Editor*
Nora Walsh, *Editorial Assistant*

Library of Congress Cataloging-in-Publication Data

Careers in Focus. Nursing
    p. cm.
  Includes index.
  ISBN 0-89434-320-3
      1. Nursing--Vocational guidance. [1. Nursing--Vocational Guidance.
2. Vocational guidance.] I. Title: Nursing. II. Ferguson Publishing Company.

RT82.C288 2000
610.73'06'9--dc21

                                                              00-037651

Printed in the United States of America

Cover photo courtesy Robert E. Daemmrich/Tony Stone Images

Published and distributed by
Ferguson Publishing Company
200 West Jackson Boulevard, 7th Floor
Chicago, Illinois 60606
800-306-9941
www.fergpubco.com

Table of
Contents

Introduction

Health Care Today

The American public is well aware of the rapid growth of managed-care programs. Because of their cost efficiency, employment opportunities in hospitals are declining, especially in administrative and support jobs. Some observers expect that consolidations and closings will reduce the number of community hospitals by as much as 10 percent in the next 10 years. Remaining hospitals are cutting costs, reducing staff, limiting the use of advanced technologies, encouraging outpatient care, and reducing paperwork.

In spite of this bleak hospital picture, the U.S. government projects that health care services will create 4.2 million new jobs by 2008. Twelve out of 30 occupations projected to grow the fastest are concentrated in health services. Registered nurses is listed as one of the top 25 occupations with fastest growth, high pay, and low unemployment.

Nursing Today

The largest group of workers in the health care field is nursing occupations, including advanced practice nurses (APNs), registered nurses (RNs), licensed practical nurses (LPNs), and nurse assistants. There are 2.5 million registered nurses in the United States, making nursing the largest sector of the health care industry, according to the National League for Nursing (NLN).

The word *nurse* comes from the Latin word *nutrire,* meaning "to nourish." The American Nurses Association (ANA) defines nursing as a combination of the art of caring and the science of health care. Those in nursing professions are concerned with particular health problems, but they also focus on patients and how they respond to treatment. Nurses are increasingly involved in wellness education, teaching people how to prevent illness and injury and avoid becoming patients.

Most nurses work directly with patients as caregivers, whether in a hospital, nursing facility, community clinic, or school. There are some, however, who spend most of their time in administrative work dealing with other nurses and medical personnel. A few work in educational settings as nursing instructors, although many instructors also work part-time with patients in hospitals or clinics.

The patient care process includes recording information about patients' physical condition, as well as psychological and sociocultural facts. It also includes determining causes of illness or injury and identifying their various stages, planning care schedules and setting treatment goals, supervising or carrying out treatment plans, and monitoring plan effectiveness. All nursing professions participate in various parts of this process, including nursing students, nurse assistants, LPNs, RNs, nurse specialists, nurse managers, and nurse instructors.

Who Are Nurses?

Nursing is extremely challenging and stressful. It is physically demanding, requiring strength, stamina, and speed. It is emotionally draining, particularly for those who work with chronically ill or dying patients. It is mentally demanding, requiring ready knowledge of techniques and procedures, keen observation skills, and meticulous attention to detail. Nurses must be able to communicate not only with patients, but also with physicians, administrators, and technicians. Their work often goes unappreciated or taken for granted. There is significant occurrence of burnout in nursing professions because of these pressures.

So who chooses a nursing profession?

Those who go into nursing soon learn about the pressures, but most find that the rewards are far greater. Nurses tend to be nurturing, caring individuals. They get great satisfaction from caring for sick or injured patients, guiding them through the healing process, and watching them respond to treatment. Nurses who care for patients with chronic or terminal illnesses find accomplishment in knowing they are providing comfort and relief from physical and emotional pain. Nurses take pride in helping people care for themselves and teaching them to prevent illness and injury. They provide a vital link between patients and other medical professionals, and often act as patient advocates and spokespersons. The health care industry could not exist without nursing professions.

Nursing has typically been a profession for Caucasian females, but that profile is rapidly changing. Today, people of all ages, ethnicities, and socioeconomic backgrounds choose nursing. According to NLN:

About 10 percent of registered nurses come from racial/ethnic minority backgrounds.

About 5.4 percent of working registered nurses are men and 13 percent of students enrolled in nursing schools are males.

The average age of registered nurses is 44.3 years.

Education and Training

Opportunities in nursing range from positions that require on-the-job training (nurse assistants), or a few months of postsecondary education (LPNs), to positions that require a master's degree or more (APNs).

According to NLN, about 35 percent of registered nurses hold an associate degree, 30 percent hold a bachelor's degree, 25 percent hold a hospital program diploma, 9 percent hold a master's degre, and less than 1 percent hold a PhD.

Not everyone chooses to pursue nursing directly after high school. Students often enter nursing later in life, as they change careers, re-enter the workforce after a hiatus, or decide to go into nursing after earning a degree in a related subject. Many nursing schools offer joint degree programs or give credit for relevant experience.

The wide variety of nursing careers allows for excellent advancement potential. With additional training a nurse assistant can become an LPN. An RN can complete extra courses and become a specialist in intensive care or surgical nursing. Many nursing schools now provide training in certain specialties as part of their regular curriculum—for example, preparing students to work with elderly patients (*geriatric nurses*) or newborns (*neonatal nurses*).

Advancement potential is also achieved through experience. Most medical facilities have a management structure that allows experienced nurses to become supervisors, managers, administrators, or instructors.

Workplaces

According to NLN, about 60 percent of employed registered nurses, or 1.3 million, work in a hospital setting. About 17 percent, or 362,648 nurses, work in community or public health settings. The *Occupational Outlook Handbook* (*OOH*) reports that about one in four hospital workers is a registered nurse.

In addition to the traditional hospital setting, nurses and nurse assistants work in nursing and personal care facilities, offices and clinics of physicians, offices and clinics of other health practitioners (chiropractors, optometrists, and podiatrists), home health care, kidney dialysis centers, drug treatment clinics, rehabilitation centers, blood banks, and schools. In some areas, advanced practice nurses are in such demand that many are opening their own practices.

Health care facilities undergo constant change. Safer, more efficient equipment and tools are being invented. Procedures are reviewed and improved. Workplaces commonly use handheld computers that record notes on each patient. Vital signs and orders for tests are then put into a database, eliminating paper and reducing record keeping errors. Nursing personnel must keep up with this flow of new information and techniques.

Workplace Issues

The *OOH* reports that in 1997, the incidence rate for occupational injury and illness in hospitals was 10 cases per 100 full-time workers, compared to an average of 7.1 in private industry. The rate was 16.2 for workers in nursing and personal care facilities.

One of the biggest concerns in nursing is the exposure to bloodborne pathogens, such as HIV (human immunodeficiency virus), HBV (hepatitis B virus), and infectious diseases, such as tuberculosis. The Centers for Disease Control reported that as of 1995, there were 151 health care workers with documented or possible work-related HIV infection and about 1,000 workers with HBV infection.

Another major concern is exposure to chemicals, such as sterilizing agents and chemotherapy drugs. Particularly at risk are nurses who work in oncology departments. Latex allergies are a risk to frequent glove users, such as surgical nurses.

Health care workers involved in direct patient care can suffer back strain from lifting patients and equipment. Home health nurses usually do not have mechanical lifting equipment that is available in hospitals, so they are more at risk for back injury and other types of overexertion when moving patients.

Most nurses have a shift work schedule that can cause a number of physical and psychological illnesses, including gastrointestinal problems, exhaustion, depression, and anxiety. The frequent changing of sleeping and eating patterns can also disrupt family routine and social life. Many nurses and nurse assistants hold more than one job, which can cause many of the same problems as shift work.

Workplace violence is an issue of concern, particularly for nurses who work in emergency rooms and psychiatric facilities.

All health care facilities must adhere to strict government and industry guidelines for safety and health practices. Following these rules and regulations significantly reduces the dangers for health care workers. Safety measures include use of safer needlestick devices, substituting less-toxic chemicals, practicing handwashing and other good hygiene, cutting down on shift rotations, use of mechanical lifting devices, and use of protective clothing, such as gloves, masks, and lead shields.

International and Volunteer Opportunities

The strong demand for nurses is not limited to the United States. There is need for nurses all over the world, and especially in developing countries struggling with overpopulation, malnutrition, infectious diseases, substance abuse, and lack of medical facilities. Nurses who choose to work in rural areas of developing countries usually do not have the equipment and medicine available in this country. Facilities can be primitive, requiring resourcefulness and flexibility. A large part of nurses' work in these situations is education—teaching basic health and wellness principles to the general population and training indigenous people as nurses.

There are also educational and cultural exchange opportunities in more developed countries. Nurses can travel to hospitals around the world to learn about other techniques, practices, and approaches to healing and caregiving.

International opportunities are most often temporary, although some nurses grow to love their adopted country and stay for their entire careers. Some arrangements include salaries, but many international assignments are volunteer. Surgical teams, community health teams, and disaster relief teams always have opportunities for volunteer nurses.

There are volunteer opportunities in the United States as well. Entry-level nurses or nurses who are re-entering the workforce after an absence can use volunteer work to gain experience. Nurses who are temporarily out of work can volunteer while they search for another position. In fact, volunteer work may lead to a paid position. Volunteer work on a resume makes a job applicant attractive to any future employer. (For more on volunteering, see the Nursing Volunteer Opportunities in Developing Nations Web site: http://www.nursingvolunteer.com/index.html)

Making a Living

Earnings are directly related to education and experience. Average salaries range from $16,600 for nurse assistants to $87,000 for nurse anesthetists. The average salaries for full-time registered nurses are about $42,071, according to NLN. Nurses have the option of working part-time, taking multiple jobs, or working for agencies to increase earning potential and allow for more flexible schedules.

The *OOH* says hospitals tend to pay the highest salaries for health service workers, followed by physician offices, and home health services. Nursing and personal care facilities pay the lowest on average.

The Future of Nursing

Employment in the health services industry is projected to increase 26 percent through 2008, compared to an average of 15 percent for all industries, reports the *OOH*. Reasons for this growth include these:

1. The elderly population will grow faster than the total population between 1998 and 2008. Their greater-than-average health care needs will increase the demand for health services, especially in home health care and nursing and personal care.
2. Advances in medical technology will continue to improve the survival rate of severely ill and injured patients, who will then need extensive therapy. New technologies often lower the cost of treatment and diagnosis, but also enable identification and treatment of conditions not previously treatable.

The *OOH* predicts that employment growth in hospitals will be the slowest within the health services industry, as it consolidates to control costs and as clinics and other alternate care sites become more common. The fastest growing job category in the industry is home health care. The government projects an 80 percent increase in these jobs by 2008.

Opportunities are excellent for APNs as they take over many of the functions of primary care physicians in the next few years, including taking patient histories and making preliminary diagnoses. Nurse practitioners are in very high demand, with recent graduates having an average of four job offers from which to choose.

The employment outlook for all kinds of nurses is very favorable. Many hospitals don't have enough nurses—the demand is much bigger than the supply. Also, as health care services expand, even more nurses will be needed. The number of RNs, at 2.08 million in 1998, is expected to increase 21.6 percent by 2008—an addition of 451,000 jobs.

Employment of LPNs is expected to increase 19.2 percent by 2008 and jobs for nursing aides and psychiatric aides are expected to increase 23.8 percent.

Careers in Focus

Each article in *Careers in Focus: Nursing* discusses a particular nursing occupation in detail. If you are interested in any of the nursing specialties, it is suggested that you first read the article, *Registered Nurses,* since earning an RN degree is a prerequisite for these specialties. All information comes from Ferguson's *Encyclopedia of Careers and Vocational Guidance,* and has been updated to include the most recent data from the latest edition of the *OOH.*

The **Overview** section gives a brief description of the career. The **History** section describes the history of the particular job as it relates to the overall development of its industry or field. **The Job** describes the primary and secondary duties of the job. **Requirements** discusses high school and postsecondary education and training requirements, any certification or licensing necessary, and any other personal requirements for success in the job. **Exploring** offers suggestions on how to gain some experience in or knowledge of the particular job before making a firm educational and financial commitment. The focus is on what can be done while still in high school (or in the early years of college) to gain a better understanding of the job. The **Employers** section gives an overview of typical places of employment for the job. **Starting Out** discusses the best ways to land that first job, be it through the college placement office, newspaper ads, or personal contact. The **Advancement** section describes what kind of career path to expect from the job and how to get there. **Earnings** lists salary ranges and describes the typical fringe benefits. The **Work Environment** section describes the typical surroundings and conditions of employment—whether indoors or outdoors, noisy or quiet, social or independent, and so on. Also discussed are typical hours worked, any seasonal fluctuations, and the stresses and strains of the job.

The **Outlook** section summarizes the job in terms of the general economy and industry projections. For the most part, Outlook information is obtained from the Bureau of Labor Statistics and is supplemented by information taken from professional associations. Job growth terms follow those used in the *OOH:* Growth described as "much faster than the average" means an increase of 36 percent or more. Growth described as "faster than the average" means an increase of 21 to 35 percent. Growth described as "about as fast as the average" means an increase of 10 to 20 percent. Growth described as "little change or more slowly than the average" means an increase of 0 to 9 percent. "Decline" means a decrease of 1 percent or more. Each article ends with **For More Information,** which lists organizations that can provide career information on training, education, internships, scholarships, and job placement.

This book also includes a list of state nursing boards, an extensive list of nursing organizations, and a job title index.

Advanced Practice Nurses

	School Subjects
Biology	
Chemistry	

Personal Skills

Helping/teaching
Technical/scientific

Work Environment

Primarily indoors
Primarily multiple locations

Minimum Education Level

Master's degree

Salary Range

$34,000 to $49,000 to $80,000

Outlook

Faster than the average

Overview

Advanced practice nurses (APNs) are a broad category of registered nurses (RNs) who have completed advanced clinical nurses' educational practice requirements beyond the two to four years of basic nursing education required for all RNs. Under the advanced practice nursing designation fall four categories of nursing specialties: *nurse practitioners* (NPs), *Certified Nurse-Midwives* (CNMs), *nurse anesthetists* or *Certified Registered Nurse Anesthetists* (CRNAs), and (CNSs). (See the separate articles on each of these specialties.)

The Job

Working in clinics, nursing homes, hospitals, and other health care settings, APNs are qualified to handle a wide range of basic health problems, usually in association with a physician, but in some cases working independently.

Specific duties of APNs are determined by their specialty and to a certain extent their precise duties are prescribed by the state in which they practice. APNs are required to be certified in 36 states and can prescribe medications in 40 states.

Working within prescribed guidelines and instructions of the physician, the APN orders, interprets, and evaluates diagnostic tests to identify the patient's clinical problems and health care needs. Then based on their findings, they record patient data and develop a treatment plan aimed at restoring the patient to health. After discussing this plan with the physician and other health professionals, they submit the plan and goals for individual patients for periodic review and evaluation. When warranted, they may prescribe (in most states) drugs or other forms of treatment such as physical therapy, inhalation therapy, and related treatments. If warranted they may refer patients to the supervising physician for consultation and their special expertise in various areas of medical practice.

Requirements

Postsecondary Training

To become an APN, the applicant must first of all become an RN (See *Registered Nurses.*). A master's degree is usually necessary to prepare for a nursing specialty or to teach. For some specialties, such as nursing research, a PhD is essential. After becoming a registered nurse, educational requirements for APNs vary depending upon the category of APN under consideration.

Certification or Licensing

Each of the four APN classifications has its own certification process. (See the separate articles on *Nurse Practitioners, Certified Nurse-Midwives, Nurse Anesthetists,* and *Clinical Nurse Specialists.*)

Exploring

You can explore your interest in the nursing field in a number of ways. You can read books on careers in nursing and talk with high school guidance counselors, school nurses, and local public health nurses. Visit hospitals to observe the work and to talk with hospital personnel.

Some hospitals now have extensive volunteer service programs in which students can work after school, on weekends, or during vacations. You can find other volunteer work experiences with the Red Cross or community health services. Camp counseling jobs sometimes offer related experiences. Some schools offer participation in Future Nurses programs.

Employers

Nurses are employed by hospitals, managed-care facilities, long-term-care facilities, clinics, industry, private homes, schools, camps, and government agencies.

Starting Out

The only way to become a registered nurse is through completion of one of the three kinds of educational programs, plus passing the licensing examination. Registered nurses may apply for employment directly to hospitals, nursing homes, companies, and government agencies that hire nurses. Jobs can also be obtained through school placement offices, by signing up with employment agencies specializing in placement of nursing personnel, or through the state employment office. Other sources of jobs include nurses' associations, professional journals, and newspaper want ads.

Advancement

Administrative and supervisory positions in the nursing field go to nurses who have earned at least the bachelor of science degree in nursing. Nurses with many years of experience who are graduates of the diploma program may achieve supervisory positions, but requirements for such promotions have become more difficult in recent years and in many cases require at least the bachelor of science in nursing degree.

Earnings

Average earnings for APNs range from $40,000 to $80,000 a year. CRNAs are at the top of the range, followed by CNSs. Salaries for CNMs and NPs are comparable. Nurses employed in private clinics of government facilities as well as those employed in hospitals and short-term care facilities enjoy attractive benefits such as paid vacations, holidays, and sick days. They often are able to participate in pension and investment programs as well as health care coverage.

Work Environment

Most hospital environments are clean and well lighted. Inner city hospitals may be in a less than desirable location and safety may be an issue. Usually, nurses work eight-hour shifts. Those in hospitals generally work any of three shifts: 7:00 AM to 3:00 PM; 3:00 PM to 11:00 PM; or 11:00 PM to 7:00 AM.

Nurses spend much of the day on their feet, either walking or standing. Handling patients who are ill or infirm can also be very exhausting. Nurses who come in contact with patients with infectious diseases must be especially careful about cleanliness and sterility. Although many nursing duties are routine, many responsibilities are unpredictable. Sick persons are often very demanding, or they may be depressed or irritable. Despite this, the nurse must retain her or his composure and should be cheerful to help the patient achieve emotional balance.

All nursing careers have some health and disease risks; however, adherence to health and safety guidelines greatly minimizes the chance of contracting infectious diseases such as hepatitis and AIDS. Medical knowledge and good safety measures are also needed to limit the nurse's exposure to toxic chemicals, radiation, and other hazards.

Outlook

While there have been some declines in the employment of advanced practice nurses in recent years, it should be noted that the demand has far outweighed the supply. In recent years, there has been a switch in health care services from inpatient surgery to outpatient surgery; hospital stays for patients are being shortened considerably by Medicare, Medicaid, and many private insurance companies. Also because of a downsizing of personnel in many corporation staffs, many persons are foregoing hospital treatment or surgery or postponing such treatment as long as possible.

Nevertheless, the federal government has predicted increasing shortages in the field for the next several years, and APNs with the proper credentials and certification should have no trouble finding posts in a wide variety of health care facilities.

For More Information

For information on accredited training programs applying to various categories of Advanced Practice Nurses, including curriculums, entrance requirements, financial assistance available, and so forth, contact the following organizations:

American Association of Nurse Anesthetists
222 South Prospect Avenue
Park Ridge, IL 60068-4001
Tel: 847-692-7050

American College of Nurse Midwives
818 Connecticut Aveune, NW, Suite 900
Washington, DC 20006
Tel: 202-728-9860

American Academy of Nurse Practitioners
PO Box 12845
Austin, TX 78711
Tel: 512-442-4262

National Alliance of Nurse Practitioners
325 Pennsylvania Avenue, SE
New York, NY 20024-2571
Tel: 202-675-6350

For information on becoming a registered nurse and for information on careers as an advanced practice nurse contact:

American Nurses Association
600 Maryland Avenue, SW, Suite 100 W
Washington, DC 20024-2571
Tel: 202-651-7000

For information on scholarships, loans, and other financial aids available to advanced practice nurses, contact:

National League for Nursing
61 Broadway, 33rd Floor
New York, NY 10006
Tel: 212-363-5555

Certified Nurse-Midwives

	School Subjects
Health Psychology Sociology	
	Personal Skills
Communication/ideas Helping/teaching	
	Minimum Education Level
Bachelor's degree	
	Salary Range
$21,580 to $45,840 to $70,100+	
	Certification or Licensing
Required by all states	
	Outlook
Faster than the average	

Overview

Certified nurse-midwives are registered nurses who assist in family planning, pregnancy, and childbirth. They also provide routine health care for women. Certified nurse-midwives work in hospitals, with physicians in private practice, in freestanding birth centers or well-woman care centers, in women's clinics, and even in the homes of clients.

History

Women have been giving birth by "natural" methods for thousands of years, since pain medication, hospitals, and medical intervention were largely unavailable until recent years. Women gave birth at home, guided by other women who were designated assistants, or midwives. *Midwife* means "with woman," and early midwives, like today's professional certified nurse-midwives (CNMs), coached mothers-to-be through their pregnancy and labor. They helped women deliver their babies and taught new mothers how to care for their infants.

In the early 1900s, however, birth was transformed from a natural event into a technological marvel. New pain medications and medical procedures took birth into the 20th century, and childbearing moved from home to hospital. Back then, midwives practiced mainly in rural areas where doctors were unavailable, or where poorer women could not afford to deliver in a hospital.

Ironically, as these medically assisted births became more prevalent in America, professional midwifery became more regulated than it had been in the past. In the early 1920s, nurse Mary Breckenridge founded the Frontier Nursing Service in eastern Kentucky to bring medical services to people in areas too poor for hospitals, as well as to women who could not afford to have their babies delivered by a high-priced doctor. After completing her midwifery training in England, she made prenatal care an additional focus of her service.

Midwife care around the world was proving itself to be both low in cost and high in quality. The Maternity Association and the Lobenstine Clinic (both in New York) established the first U.S. midwifery school and graduated its first class in 1933. In the mid-1930s, the Frontier Nursing Service opened its own nurse-midwifery school, and it remains today the oldest continuing U.S. midwifery program.

During the next few decades, most women who were able to deliver in a hospital preferred the lull of pain medication and the perceived safety of the medical establishment, and midwifery remained a tool of poor and rural women. Pregnancy and childbirth were considered medical procedures best left in the hands of obstetricians and gynecologists. Both the medical community and the public have generally frowned upon midwifery in favor of doctors and hospitals.

Since the 1960s, however, this attitude has been changing as more women insist on more natural methods of giving birth. In 1968, the American College of Nurse-Midwives (ACNM), the premier midwife organization in the United States, was established. This creation of a nationally standardized entity to regulate midwife training and practice introduced midwifery as a positive, healthy, and safe alternative to hospital births. The nurse-midwife, officially known as a certified nurse-midwife (CNM), has gradually become accepted as a respected member of the health care teams involved with family planning, pregnancy, and labor.

A number of studies have indicated that babies delivered by nurse-midwives are less likely to experience low birth weights and other health complications than babies delivered by physicians. In fact, a recent study from the National Center for Health Statistics, Centers for Disease Control and Prevention, indicates that the risk of death for the baby during birth was 19 percent lower for CNM-assisted deliveries than for physician-attended births.

The proven safety standards of births attended by nurse-midwives, the cost-effectiveness of a CNM-assisted pregnancy and labor, and the personal touch that many women get from their nurse-midwives will ensure that CNMs become vital links between traditional birthing practices and the high-tech worlds of today and tomorrow.

The Job

Nurse-midwives examine pregnant women and monitor the growth and development of fetuses. Typically a nurse-midwife is responsible for all phases of a normal pregnancy, including prenatal care, assisting during labor, and providing follow-up care. A certified nurse-midwife always works in consultation with a physician, who can be called upon should complications arise during pregnancy or childbirth. Nurse-midwives can provide emergency assistance to their patients while physicians are called. In most states, nurse-midwives are authorized to prescribe and administer medications. Many nurse-midwives provide the full spectrum of women's health care, including regular gynecological exams and well-woman care.

Not all midwives are certified nurse-midwives. Most states recognize other categories of midwives, including direct-entry (or licensed) midwives, certified professional midwives (CPMs), and lay (or empirical) midwives.

Direct-entry midwives are not required to be nurses in order to practice as midwives. They typically assist in home births or at birthing centers and are trained through a combination of formal education, apprenticeship, and self-education. Direct-entry midwives are legally recognized in 29 states that offer licensing, certification, or registration programs, and they perform most of the services of CNMs. Although they generally have professional relationships with physicians, hospitals, and laboratories to provide support and emergency services, few direct-entry midwives actually practice in medical centers.

Certified professional midwives (CPMs) must meet the basic requirements of the North American Registry of Midwives (NARM). Potential CPMs must pass a written examination and an assessment of their skills, and they must have proven training assisting in out-of-hospital births. NARM accepts various midwifery programs and practical apprenticeship as a basis for certification.

Lay midwives usually train by apprenticing with established midwives, although some may acquire formal education as well. Lay midwives are not certified or licensed, either because they lack the necessary experience and education or because they pursue nontraditional childbirth techniques. Many lay midwives practice only as part of religious communities or specific ethnic groups, and typically assist only in home birth situations. Some states have made it illegal for lay midwives to charge for their services.

Since the education and certification standards for direct-entry midwives, certified professional midwives, and lay midwives vary from state to state, the rest of this article will deal only with certified nurse-midwives, who must complete a core nursing curriculum—as well as midwifery training—to become midwives. When the terms "nurse-midwife" and "midwife" are used in this article, certified nurse-midwife is implied.

Deborah Woolley has been a registered nurse since 1975 and has been practicing as a nurse-midwife since 1983. For Woolley, midwifery offered her the opportunity to have a positive impact on women's health care and childbirth experiences. "I started out as a nurse assigned to the labor and delivery unit. But I became frustrated with the type of care the women were getting," Woolley says. "You'll find that a lot among midwives. Most of the midwives I talk to can point to an event that was the straw that broke the camel's back, as it were—when they realized that they wanted to have more influence over the experience the woman is having. Midwifery's focus is on improving conditions for women and their families. In a way, midwifery is a radical departure from the old way of looking at pregnancy."

Woolley typically arrives at the hospital at 7:00 AM and spends the first hour or more seeing patients in postpartum—that is, women who have given birth the day or night before. At about 8:30 AM, Woolley goes down to the clinic to begin seeing other patients. "I work a combination of full days and half days during the week. On a half day, I'll see patients for four hours and work on paperwork for one hour. On a full day, I'll see patients for eight hours and work on paperwork for two hours," Woolley says. "But that doesn't mean I always leave exactly at five o'clock. At the clinic, we see everyone who shows up."

After Woolley meets a new patient, she'll spend an hour or so taking the patient's medical history, examining her, and getting her scheduled into the prenatal care system. "I also ask about a patient's life. I spend time with the patient and try to get to know her and what's going on in her life. It makes a big difference in the care she's provided. I think one of the things that makes midwives so effective is that they really get to know their patients."

An important part of a certified nurse-midwife's work is the education of patients. Nurse-midwives teach their patients about proper nutrition and fitness for healthy pregnancies and about different techniques for labor and delivery. Nurse-midwives also counsel their patients in the postpartum period about breast-feeding, parenting, and other areas concerning the health of mother and child. Nurse-midwives provide counseling on several other issues, including sexually transmitted diseases, spousal and child abuse, and social support networks. In some cases, this counseling may extend to family members of the soon-to-be or new mother, or even to older siblings of the family's newest addition. Woolley believes that this education is one of a midwife's key responsibilities. "I spend a lot of time teaching things like nutrition, the process of fetal development, and basic parenting skills. I'll refer patients to Lamaze classes. I'll also screen patients for family problems, such as violence in the home, and teach them how to get out of abusive situations," Woolley says. "In other words, I'll teach a patient anything she needs to know if she's pregnant. I try to empower women to take charge of their own health care and their own lives."

Apart from seeing patients, Woolley is also responsible for maintaining patient records. "I have to review lab results and ultrasounds and fill out birth certificates—things like that," she says. "There's a lot of writing involved, too. I have to document everything that I do with patients, including what I've done and how and why I've done it." This may include recording patient information, filing documents and patient charts, doing research to find out why a woman is having a particular problem, and consulting with physicians and other medical personnel. Many midwives build close relationships with their patients and try to be available for their patients at any time of the day or night.

Requirements

High School

In high school, you should begin preparing for a career as a nurse-midwife by taking a broad range of college preparatory courses, with a focus on science classes. Anatomy, biology, and chemistry will give you solid background information for what you will be studying in college. Additional classes in sociology and psychology will help you learn how to deal with a variety of patients from different ethnic and economic groups. English and business classes will teach you how to deal with the paperwork involved in any profession. Finally, you should consider learning foreign languages if you want to serve as a midwife to immigrant communities.

Postsecondary Training

All certified nurse-midwives begin their careers as registered nurses. In order to become a registered nurse, you will need to graduate from either a four-year bachelor's degree program in nursing or a two-year associate's degree program in nursing. After receiving a degree, you can apply for admission into an accredited certificate program in nurse-midwifery or an accredited master's degree program in nurse-midwifery.

With an associate's degree in nursing, you will be eligible for acceptance into a nurse-midwifery certificate program. A certificate program typically requires nine to 12 months of study. In order to be accepted into a master's degree program in nurse-midwifery, you must first earn your bachelor's degree in nursing. A master's degree program requires 16 to 24 months of study. Some master's degree programs also require one year of clinical experience in order to earn a nurse-midwife degree. In these programs, the prospective nurse-midwife is trained to provide primary care services, gynecological care, preconception and prenatal care, labor delivery and management, and postpartum and infant care.

Procedures that nurse-midwives are trained to perform include physical examinations, pap smears, and episiotomies. They may also repair incisions from cesarean sections, administer anesthesia, and prescribe medications. Nurse-midwives are trained to provide counseling on subjects such as nutrition, breastfeeding, and infant care. Nurse-midwives learn to provide both physical and emotional support to pregnant women and their families.

Certification or Licensing

After earning either a midwifery certificate from a nationally accredited nurse-midwifery program or a master's degree in midwifery, midwives are required to take a national examination administered by the American College of Nurse-Midwives (ACNM). Upon passing the exam, the new midwife achieves full endorsement as a medical professional, as well as the title "certified nurse-midwife." Those who have passed this examination are licensed to practice nurse-midwifery in all 50 states. Each state, however, has its own laws and regulations governing the activities and responsibilities of nurse-midwives.

Other Requirements

If you are interested in becoming a certified nurse-midwife, you will need skills that aren't necessarily taught in midwifery programs. Nurse-midwives need to enjoy working with people, learning about their patients' needs, and helping them through a very important life change. They should be sympathetic to the needs of their patients. They need to be independent and able to accept responsibility for their actions and decisions. Strong observation skills are key, as nurse-midwives must be tuned into their patients' needs during pregnancy and labor. Nurse-midwives also need to listen well and respond appropriately. They must communicate effectively with patients, family members, physicians, and other hospital staff, as well as insurance company personnel. Finally, nurse-midwives should be confident and composed, responding well in an emergency and keeping their patients calm.

Exploring

Volunteer work as a "candy striper" at your local hospital or clinic may put you in contact with nurse-midwives who can help you learn more about midwifery. You might also volunteer to visit and offer emotional support to laboring mothers-to-be at a hospital or freestanding birth center.

You may wish to contact a professional midwifery organization for more information about the field. These associations often publish journals or newsletters to keep members informed of new issues in midwifery. The better known organizations may have Web sites that can give you more information about midwifery in your area. A list of some organizations is at the end of this article.

Finally, young women may wish to see a nurse-midwife in lieu of a physician for their well-woman care. Although nurse-midwives are usually thought of in conjunction with pregnancy, many women use nurse-midwives as their primary medical contact from their teenage years through menopause.

Employers

Hospitals are the primary source of employment for certified nurse-midwives. Approximately 85 percent of the more than 6,500 nurse-midwives in the United States work in hospitals. They see patients and attend deliveries on hospital grounds and use hospital-owned equipment for examinations and other procedures. Additional medical personnel are always available for emergency situations. Most of the remaining nurse-midwives work in family planning clinics and other health care clinics and privately funded agencies. These nurse-midwives usually have relationships with specific hospitals and physicians in case of an emergency. Finally, some nurse-midwives operate their own clinics and birthing centers, while others work independently and specialize in home birth deliveries.

Starting Out

Woolley earned a bachelor's degree in nursing and then began her career as a nurse at a labor and delivery unit in a Texas hospital. While working, she attended graduate school and earned a master's degree in maternal child nursing. She then went to Chicago, where she began training as a nurse-midwife. "After earning my nurse-midwifery degree," Woolley says, "I heard there were openings at Cook County Hospital here in Chicago. So I applied for a job there. What I liked about Cook County was that they continued to train me while I was working. They gave me assertiveness training and training in urban health issues."

Like Woolley, most certified nurse-midwives finish their formal education in nursing and midwifery before beginning work. They usually have some opportunities to work with patients as a student. Beginning midwives may also intern at a hospital or clinic to fulfill class requirements.

Certified nurse-midwives can begin their careers in various ways. Some may move from an internship to a full-time job when they complete their education requirements at a certain facility. Others may seek out a position through a professional midwifery organization or try for a job at a specific location that interests them. Finally, some nurse-midwives begin by working as nurses in other areas of health care and then move into midwifery as opportunities become available.

Advancement

With experience, a nurse-midwife can advance into a supervisory role or into an administrative capacity at a hospital, family planning clinic, birthing center, or other facility. Many nurse-midwives, like Woolley, choose to continue their education and complete PhD programs. With a doctorate, a nurse-midwife can do research or teaching. "I spent four-and-a-half years at Cook County while I was working on my PhD," Woolley says. "From there I was recruited to Colorado to head up the midwifery unit at a hospital there. After six years as a director in Colorado, I learned that the director's position here at UIC was open, and I jumped at the chance to come back to Chicago."

Nurse-midwives with advanced degrees may choose to move away from the day-to-day patient care and write for journals or magazines. They may also lean more toward the research aspects of prenatal care and obstetrics. Finally, nurse-midwives may prefer to apply their experience and education and move toward other areas of medicine or hospital administration.

Earnings

According to the Association of Certified Nurse-Midwives, salaries range from $40,000 to $70,000. CNMs are among the highest paid nursing professionals. Starting salaries for beginning nurse-midwives can range from $21,580 to around $45,000 per year, depending on the place of employment; those working for large hospitals tend to earn more than those working for small hospitals, clinics, and birthing centers. The most experienced nurse-midwives, including those in supervisory, director, and administrative positions, can earn much more. Salaries also vary according to the region of the country and whether the employing facility is private or public.

Nurse-midwives generally enjoy a good benefits package, although these too can vary widely depending on employer. CNMs working in hospitals or well-established clinics or birthing centers usually receive a full complement of benefits, including medical coverage, paid sick time, and holiday and vacation pay. They may also be able to work a more flexible schedule to accommodate family or personal obligations.

Work Environment

Nurse-midwives who work in hospitals or as part of a physician's practice work indoors in clean, professional surroundings. Although most nurse-midwives perform checkups and routine visits alone with their patients, a number of other health care professionals are on hand in case the midwife has a question or needs assistance in an emergency. Nurse-midwives often consult with doctors, medical insurance representatives, and family members of their patients, as well as other midwives in order to determine the best care routine for the women they serve.

In a hospital, CNMs usually wear professional clothing, a lab coat, and comfortable shoes to allow for plenty of running around during the day. They often wear hospital scrubs during delivery. In a free-standing birth center, the nurse-midwives may have a more casual dress code but still maintain a professional demeanor.

Midwives try to make their offices and birthing areas as calm and as reassuring as possible so their patients feel comfortable during checkups and delivery. Soft music may play in the background, or the waiting area may be decorated like a nursery and filled with parenting magazines.

Although most nurse-midwives work a 40-hour week, these hours may not reflect the typical nine-to-five day, since babies are delivered at all hours of the day and night. Many hospitals or clinics offer nurse-midwives a more flexible schedule in exchange for having the CNM "on-call" for births.

Finally, although there are no gender requirements in the profession, nurse-midwifery is a field dominated by women. Well over 98 percent of CNMs in the United States are female. Women have traditionally helped each other through pregnancy and delivery. Just as women who became doctors 100 years ago had to overcome many barriers, men considering entering midwifery should be prepared for hurdles of their own.

Outlook

The number of nurse-midwifery jobs is expected to grow faster than the average for all occupations through 2008, as nurse-midwives gain a reputation as an integral part of the health care community. Currently, there are more positions than there are CNMs to fill them. This situation is expected to continue for the near future.

There are two factors driving the demand for nurse-midwives. The first element is the growth of interest in natural childbearing techniques among women. The number of midwife-assisted births has risen dramatically since the 1970s. Some women have been attracted to midwifery because of studies that indicate natural childbirth is more healthful for mother and child than doctor-assisted childbirth. Other women have been attracted to midwifery because it emphasizes the participation of the entire family in prenatal care and labor.

The second factor in the growing demand for nurse-midwives is economic. As society moves toward managed care programs and the health care community emphasizes cost-effectiveness, midwifery should increase in popularity. This is because the care provided by nurse-midwives costs substantially less than the care provided by obstetricians and gynecologists. If the cost advantage of midwifery continues, more insurers and health maintenance organizations will probably direct patients to certified nurse-midwives for care.

For More Information

This organization is the largest and most widely known midwifery organization in the United States. For more information about the midwife certification process, contact:

American College of Nurse-Midwives
818 Connecticut Avenue, NW, Suite 900
Washington, DC 20006
Tel: 202-728-9860
Web: http://www.midwife.org/ or http://www.acnm.org/

The following organizations can give you information about all types of midwifery:

Midwives Alliance of North America
Tel: 888-923-MANA (6262)
Web: http://www.mana.org/

For a list of nursing programs, contact:

American Association of Colleges of Nursing
1 Dupont Circle, NW, Suite 530
Washington, DC 20036
Tel: 202-463-6930
Web: http://www.aacn.nche.edu/

Clinical Nurse Specialists

Biology Chemistry	School Subjects
Helping/teaching Technical/scientific	Personal Skills
Primarily indoors Primarily one location	Work Environment
Master's degree	Minimum Education Level
$35,000 to $47,600 to $80,000	Salary Range
Required by all states	Certification or Licensing
Faster than the average	Outlook

Overview

Clinical Nurse Specialist (CNS), a classification of *advanced practice nurses* (APNs), are registered nurses who have completed advanced clinical nurses' educational practice requirements. Qualified to handle a wide variety of physical and mental health problems, CNSs are primarily involved in providing primary health care and psychotherapy.

The Job

CNSs conduct health assessments and evaluations based on the patient's history, laboratory tests, and their own personal examinations. Following such assessments they arrive at a diagnosis of the patient's problem and deliver care and develop quality control methods to help correct the patient's medical problem. In addition to delivering direct patient care, CNSs may be involved in consultation, research, education, and administration. They may specialize in one or more areas, such as pediatrics, mental health, perinatal care, oncology, or gerontology. A few work independently or in private practice and are qualified for reimbursement by Medicare, Medicaid, and other federally sponsored or private health care payers.

Requirements

Postsecondary Training

CNSs must earn a master's or higher degree after completing their studies for their RN. (See *Registered Nurses* and *Advanced Practice Nurses*.) Many CNSs go on to earn their doctoral degrees. CNSs can specialize by focusing their studies in a specific area, such as community health, home health, gerontology, or medical-surgical.

Certification or Licensing

CNS certification is available through the American Nurses Association. Applicants must have completed education and experience requirements before taking the certification test.

Exploring

You can explore your interest in the nursing field in a number of ways. You can read books on careers in nursing and talk with high school guidance counselors, school nurses, and local public health nurses. Visit hospitals to observe the work and to talk with hospital personnel.

Some hospitals now have extensive volunteer service programs in which students can work after school, on weekends, or during vacations. You can find other volunteer work experiences with the Red Cross or community health services. Camp counseling jobs sometimes offer related experiences. Some schools offer participation in Future Nurses programs.

Employers

Nurses are employed by hospitals, managed-care facilities, long-term-care facilities, clinics, industry, private homes, schools, camps, and government agencies.

Starting Out

The only way to become a registered nurse is through completion of one of the three kinds of educational programs, plus passing the licensing examination. Registered nurses may apply for employment directly to hospitals, nursing homes, companies, and government agencies that hire nurses. Jobs can also be obtained through school placement offices, by signing up with employment agencies specializing in placement of nursing personnel, or through the state employment office. Other sources of jobs include nurses' associations, professional journals, and newspaper want ads.

Advancement

Administrative and supervisory positions in the nursing field go to nurses who have earned at least the bachelor of science degree in nursing. Nurses with many years of experience who are graduates of the diploma program may achieve supervisory positions, but requirements for such promotions have become more difficult in recent years and in many cases require at least the bachelor of science in nursing degree.

Earnings

Salary figures for the various categories of APNs are based on total salary income as well as earnings from working overtime and while on-call. According to the U.S. Labor Department, CNSs average $47,674.

In addition, nurses employed in private clinics or government facilities as well as those employed in hospitals and short-term care facilities enjoy attractive benefits, such as paid vacations, holidays, and sick days, and quite often participation in pension and investment programs as well as health care coverage not only for themselves but for their families as well.

Work Environment

CNSs work primarily in hospitals, clinics, or nursing homes but may work out of their own homes and other community-based settings, including industry, home health care, and HMOs.

Outlook

While there have been some declines in the employment of advanced practice nurses in recent years, it should be noted that the demand has far outweighed the supply. The federal government has predicted increasing shortages in the field for the next several years, and advanced practice nurses with the proper credentials and certification should have no trouble finding posts in a wide variety of health care facilities.

For More Information

National Association of Clinical Nurse Specialists
4700 West Lake Avenue
Glenview, IL 60025
Tel: 847-375-4740
Email: info@nacns.org
Web: http://www.nacns.org/

Community Health Nurses

	School Subjects
Biology	
Chemistry	
	Personal Interests
Helping/teaching	
Technical/scientific	
	Work Environment
Primarily indoors	
Primarily multiple locations	
	Minimum Education Level
Some postsecondary training	
	Salary Range
$22,000 to $30,000 to $70,000	
	Certification or Licensing
Required by all states	
	Outlook
Faster than the average	

Overview

Community health nurses provide community-based health care. They organize, promote, and deliver care to community groups in urban, rural, and remote settings. They may work in community health centers in large and small cities, or they may travel to remote locations to bring health care treatment and information to people living in those areas. They may provide public health services and educational programs to schools, correctional facilities, homeless shelters, elderly care facilities, and maternal and well-baby clinics. Some community health nurses provide specialized care in communities where immediate physician services are not available. Community health nurses often work for a state- or federally-funded agency, or a private health provider company.

The Job

Community health nurses work with many aspects of a community's population. Their duties vary greatly depending on their locale and assignments. Some community health nurses may instruct a class for expectant mothers, visit new parents to help them learn how to care for their new baby, talk with senior citizens about exercise and nutrition, or give immunizations at a community center or other site. Other community health nurses may travel to remote areas where health care is not readily available. Here they may work with a medical doctor or nurse practitioner to provide necessary medical care and health education. Community health nurses usually work with all ages, ranging in age from birth to the elderly. They also may work with different groups of people, including immigrants, homeless shelter residents, and persons who are developmentally or physically challenged.

Community health nurses may also be educators who plan, promote, and administer community-wide wellness programs. They may also give presentations to area organizations, schools, and health care facilities regarding health, safety, exercise, and nutrition.

Some community health nurses may work with managed care providers and provide HMO-sponsored programs to the plan's members or to the community.

As with almost all health care professions today, community health nurses spend a great deal of time keeping records and charts, and documenting the services they provide in order to meet insurance, government, and Medicare requirements.

Requirements

Postsecondary Training

Nurses who specialize in a specific nursing field such as a community health nurse must first become registered nurses. (See *Registered Nurses*.) Many community health nurses are required to have some general nursing experience since they may be required to work with patients with a wide range of health problems. Entry-level requirements depend on the employing agency and the availability of nurses in that specialty and geographical region.

Certification or Licensing

Certification is a voluntary process. Nurses who wish to specialize in community health care may choose to attend graduate school.

Other Requirements

Community health nurses should feel comfortable working with all ages and people from all cultural backgrounds. Good communication skills are essential, including the ability to listen and respond to the patient's needs. Flexibility is also a requirement since duties vary greatly from hour to hour and day to day. Community health nurses must be able to work independently, have good organizational skills, and also have the ability to supervise aides and other support people.

Exploring

You can explore your interest in the nursing field in a number of ways. You can read books on careers in nursing and talk with high school guidance counselors, school nurses, and local public health nurses. Visit hospitals to observe the work and to talk with hospital personnel.

Some hospitals now have extensive volunteer service programs in which students can work after school, on weekends, or during vacations. You can find other volunteer work experiences with the Red Cross or community health services. Camp counseling jobs sometimes offer related experiences. Some schools offer participation in Future Nurses programs.

Employers

Nurses are employed by hospitals, managed-care facilities, long-term-care facilities, clinics, industry, private homes, schools, camps, and government agencies.

Starting Out

The only way to become a registered nurse is through completion of one of the three kinds of educational programs, plus passing the licensing examination. Registered nurses may apply for employment directly to hospitals, nursing homes, companies, and government agencies that hire nurses. Jobs can also be obtained through school placement offices, by signing up with employment agencies specializing in placement of nursing personnel, or through the state employment office. Other sources of jobs include nurses' associations, professional journals, and newspaper want ads.

Advancement

Administrative and supervisory positions in the nursing field go to nurses who have earned at least the bachelor of science degree in nursing. Nurses with many years of experience who are graduates of the diploma program may achieve supervisory positions, but requirements for such promotions have become more difficult in recent years and in many cases require at least the bachelor of science in nursing degree.

Earnings

According to the U.S. Department of Labor's *Occupational Outlook Handbook,* registered nurses earned an average of $40,690 annually in 1998. The low 10 percent earned less than $29,480, while the middle 50 percent earned between $34,430 and $49,070. The top 10 percent made over $69,300 a year.

Salary is determined by many factors, including nursing specialty, education, place of employment, geographical location, and work experience. Flexible schedules are available for most full-time nurses. Employers usually provide health and life insurance, and some offer educational reimbursements and year-end bonuses to their full-time staff.

Work Environment

Working environments vary depending on the community health nurse's responsibilities. Some community health nurses may work in clean, well-lighted buildings in upscale communities, while others may find themselves working in remote, underdeveloped areas that have poor living conditions. Personal safety may be an issue at times. Some community health nurses may also work overseas in government or private enterprises.

All nursing careers have some health and disease risks; however, adherence to health and safety guidelines greatly minimizes the chance of contracting infectious diseases such as hepatitis and AIDS. Medical knowledge and good safety measures are also needed to limit the nurse's exposure to toxic chemicals, radiation, and other hazards.

Outlook

Nursing specialties will be in great demand in the future. The U.S. Bureau of Labor Statistics lists nursing as one of 10 occupations with the largest growth rate. From 1998 to 2008, jobs in nursing are expected to increase by 21.6 percent. In addition, the unemployment rate for all nursing professions reported by the American Association of Critical Care Nurses (AACN) is less than 2 percent. Part-time job opportunities are also plentiful in the nursing profession.

The outlook for community health nurses is excellent. The U.S. Bureau of the Census estimates that the number of individuals aged 65 or older will double by 2050. As our population grows older, the need for community-based nursing will increase. In addition, managed care organizations will continue to need community health nurses to provide health promotion and disease prevention programs to their subscribers.

For More Information

American Association of Colleges of Nursing
One Dupont Circle, Suite 530
Washington, DC 20036
Tel: 202-463-6930
Web: http://www.aacn.nche.edu

Association of Community Health Nursing Educators
7794 Grow Drive
Pensacola, FL 32514-7072
Tel: 850-474-8821
Email: ACHNE@puetzamc.com

Critical Care Nurses

School Subjects
- Biology
- Chemistry

Personal Interests
- Helping/teaching
- Technical/scientific

Work Environment
- Primarily indoors
- Primarily one location

Minimum Education Level
- Some postsecondary training

Salary Range
- $30,000 to $50,000 to $75,000

Certification or Licensing
- Required by all states

Outlook
- Faster than the average

Overview

Critical care nurses provide highly skilled direct patient care to critically ill patients needing intense medical treatment. Contrary to previously held beliefs that critical care nurses work only in intensive care units (ICU) or cardiac care units (CCU) of hospitals, today's critical care nurses work in the emergency departments, post anesthesia recovery units, pediatric intensive care units, burn units, and neonatal intensive care units of medical facilities, as well as in other units that treat critically ill patients.

The Job

Critical care nursing is a very challenging job. Because medical facilities employ critical care nurses who work in various units, their job responsibilities vary; however, their main responsibility is providing highly skilled medical care for critically ill patients. Critical care nurses may be assigned one or two patients that they care for as opposed to being involved in the care of several patients.

Brandon Frady, a registered nurse and a certified critical care nurse, works in the pediatrics intensive care unit of an Atlanta children's hospital. He works as a bedside nurse and as a relief charge nurse meaning that he is not only responsible for caring for his patients, but that he is also in charge of the administration of the ward.

Frady is also part of the ground transport team that transports critically ill or injured children within a 150-mile radius to their center. "We are the cutting edge hospital for pediatric health care," says Frady. "We care for very sick children here and our skills are challenged on a daily basis."

Critical care nursing means keeping up with the latest medical technology and research as well as medical treatments and procedures. "There is something new to learn every day," Frady says. "We have to learn to operate very high tech machines and we are frequently tested on their use and operation. Plus, we need to know the latest research and treatments available for acutely ill children."

Critical care nursing is a very intense nursing specialty. Patients require constant care and monitoring, says Brandon. "Many hospitals are requiring nurses to work 12-hour shifts, which can be very exhausting."

In many cases, critical care nurses are confronted with situations that require them to act immediately on the patients' behalf. The nurse must be a patient advocate meaning that the nurse must help the patients receive the best possible care and also respect their wishes. They must also provide support and education to the patients and their families.

"Although it can be an emotionally draining job, it can also be very rewarding to know that I helped the child and family get through their medical crisis," Frady relates. "It is especially satisfying when they come back later and thank you for what you have done. The job has a lot of satisfaction."

Requirements

Postsecondary Training

Critical care nurses must be registered nurses. (See *Registered Nurses*.) Entry-level requirements to become a critical care nurse depend on the institution, its size, who it serves, and the availability of nurses in that specialty and geographical region. Usually nurses must have some bedside nursing experience before entering the critical care nursing field. However, some hospitals are developing graduate internship and orientation programs that allow new graduates to enter this specialty.

Certification or Licensing

There are critical care nursing certification programs available through the American Association of Critical-Care Nurses (AACRN). Some institutions may require certification as a critical care nurse.

Other Requirements

Critical care nurses should like working in a fast-paced environment that requires life-long learning. This is a very intense nursing field and nurses should be able to make critical decisions quickly and intelligently. New medical technology is constantly being developed and implemented. Critical care nurses should be technically inclined and able to learn how to operate new medical equipment without feeling intimidated.

Critical care nurses must be able to deal with major life and death crises. Because of the seriousness of their loved one's illness, family members and friends may be difficult to deal with and the nurse must display patience, understanding, and composure during these emotional times. The nurse must be able to communicate with the family and explain medical terminology and procedures to the patient and family so they can understand what is being done and why.

Exploring

You can explore your interest in the nursing field in a number of ways. You can read books on careers in nursing and talk with high school guidance counselors, school nurses, and local public health nurses. Visit hospitals to observe the work and to talk with hospital personnel.

Some hospitals now have extensive volunteer service programs in which students can work after school, on weekends, or during vacations. You can find other volunteer work experiences with the Red Cross or community health services. Camp counseling jobs sometimes offer related experiences. Some schools offer participation in Future Nurses programs.

Employers

Nurses are employed by hospitals, managed-care facilities, long-term-care facilities, clinics, industry, private homes, schools, camps, and government agencies.

Starting Out

The only way to become a registered nurse is through completion of one of the three kinds of educational programs, plus passing the licensing examination. Registered nurses may apply for employment directly to hospitals, nursing homes, companies, and government agencies that hire nurses. Jobs can also be obtained through school placement offices, by signing up with employment agencies specializing in placement of nursing personnel, or through the state employment office. Other sources of jobs include nurses' associations, professional journals, and newspaper want ads.

Advancement

Administrative and supervisory positions in the nursing field go to nurses who have earned at least the bachelor of science degree in nursing. Nurses with many years of experience who are graduates of the diploma program may achieve supervisory positions, but requirements for such promotions have become more difficult in recent years and in many cases require at least the bachelor of science in nursing degree.

Earnings

According to the U.S. Department of Labor's *Occupational Outlook Handbook,* registered nurses earned an average of $40,690 annually in 1998. The low 10 percent earned less than $29,480, while the middle 50 percent earned between $34,430 and $49,070. The top 10 percent made over $69,300 a year. However, critical care nurses in certain areas may earn more.

Salary is determined by many factors, including nursing specialty, education, and place of employment, shift worked, geographical location, and work experience. Flexible schedules and part-time employment opportunities are available for most nurses. Employers usually provide health and life insurance, and some offer educational reimbursements and year-end bonuses to their full-time staff.

Work Environment

Most critical-care nurses work in hospitals in the intensive care unit (ICU), the emergency department, the operating room, or some other specialty unit. Most hospital environments are clean and well lighted. Inner city hospitals may be in a less than desirable location and safety may be an issue. Generally, critical-care nurses who wish to advance in their careers will find themselves working in larger hospitals or medical centers in major cities.

All nursing careers have some health and disease risks; however, adherence to health and safety guidelines greatly minimizes the chance of contracting infectious diseases such as hepatitis and AIDS. Medical knowledge and good safety measures are also needed to limit the nurse's exposure to toxic chemicals, radiation, and other hazards.

Outlook

Nursing specialties will be in great demand in the future. The U.S. Bureau of Labor Statistics lists nursing as one of 10 occupations with the largest growth rate. From 1998 to 2008, jobs for registered nurses are expected to increase by 21.6 percent. In addition, the unemployment rate for all nursing professions according to AACN is less than 2 percent.

According to the American Association of Critical-Care Nurses, a growing number of hospitals are experiencing a shortage of critical care nurses. Many hospitals needing critical care nurses are offering incentives such as sign-on bonuses. The most critical shortages are in areas that require nurses with experience and highly specialized skills. The highest increase in demand is for those critical care nurses who specialize in a specific area of care, i.e., cardiovascular ICU, pediatric and neonatal ICU, and open-heart recovery units. Job opportunities vary across the country and may be available in all geographic areas and in large and small hospitals.

For More Information

American Association of Colleges of Nursing
One Dupont Circle, NW, Suite 530
Washington, DC 20036
Tel: 202-463-6930
Web: http://www.aacn.nche.edu

American Association of Critical-Care Nurses
101 Columbia
Aliso Viejo, CA 92656-1491
Tel: 800-899-2226
Web: http://www.aacn.org

Emergency Nurses

	School Subjects
Biology Chemistry	

	Personal Interests
Helping/teaching Technical/scientific	

	Work Environment
Primarily indoors Primarily one location	

	Minimum Education Level
Some postsecondary training	

	Salary Range
$29,000 to $49,000 to $69,000	

	Certification or Licensing
Required by all states	

	Outlook
Faster than the average	

Overview

Emergency nurses provide highly skilled direct patient care to people who need emergency treatment for an illness or injury. Emergency nurses incorporate all the specialties of nursing. They care for infant, pediatric, adult, and elderly patients with a broad spectrum of medical needs.

The Job

Emergency nursing is a very challenging job. The main responsibility of emergency nurses is to provide highly skilled emergency medical care for patients. Although emergency nursing is its own nursing specialty, it incorporates almost every other nursing specialty in the profession. Emergency nurses deal with pregnant women, newborn babies, patients with cancer, children, accident victims, AIDS patients, Alzheimer patients, the elderly, cardiac arrest patients, and psychologically disturbed and violent people. Emergency care can range from giving general nursing care to someone with a severe case of the flu, to performing life- and limb-saving procedures.

When a patient enters the emergency facility, the nurses must first assess the patient and determine the immediacy of the illness or injury. This includes a quick preliminary diagnosis and assessment of the overall condition of the patient. They talk to the patient and family. They also record vital signs and observe the patient's symptoms or check for injuries that may not be readily visible.

Emergency nurses must prioritize their patients' needs, especially if it is a triage situation, such as a disaster or accident involving a number of people who require treatment. They must be able to stabilize the patient; prepare the patient for emergency testing, laboratory procedures, or surgery; and perform resuscitation, if necessary. In many instances the nurse will have to perform initial treatments until a doctor can see the patient. This may include setting up or using high-tech medical equipment.

In many cases, emergency nurses are confronted with situations that require them to act immediately, independently, and confidently. But, they must be a good team player. They must work with other medical, administrative, and law enforcement personnel in what can become a very tense and emotional situation.

Often emergency nurses must be patient advocates, meaning that they must help the patient receive the best possible care and also respect the patient's wishes regarding treatment. Nurses must be in touch with the family during the emergency crisis and help them deal with their emotions and fears.

Not only are emergency nurses required to attend to the physical needs of patients, they may be involved in crisis intervention in some cases such as homelessness, sexual assault, domestic violence, or child abuse.

Emergency nurses must also act as educators. Many people who are seen in emergency care facilities do not have access to follow-up care so nurses must educate their patients about self-care when they are discharged. This may include showing them how to care for their wounds or injuries or recommending lifestyle changes, if necessary, to adapt to their conditions or plans of treatment.

Requirements

Postsecondary Training

Emergency nurses must be registered nurses. (See *Registered Nurses.*) Entry-level requirements to become an emergency nurse depend on the state, the institution, its size, who it serves, and the availability of nurses in that specialty and geographical region. Usually nurses must have some nursing experience before entering the emergency-nursing field.

Certification or Licensing

Some institutions may require certification as an emergency room nurse. Certification is available through the Board of Certification for Emergency Nursing (BCEN) and requires recertification every four years.

Other Requirements

Emergency room nurses should like working in a fast-paced environment that requires life-long learning. This is a very intense nursing field and nurses should be able to make critical decisions quickly and intelligently. New medical technology is constantly being developed and implemented. Emergency care nurses should be technically inclined and skilled in operating medical equipment.

Emergency nurses must be able to deal with major life and death crises. Because of the suddenness and perhaps seriousness of their loved one's illness, family members and friends may be difficult to deal with and the nurse must display patience, understanding, and composure during these emotional times. The nurse must be able to communicate with the family and explain medical terminology and procedures to the patient and family so they can understand what is being done and why.

Emergency nursing is a very intense nursing specialty. Patients require immediate attention, constant care, and monitoring, and many facilities are requiring nurses to work 12-hour shifts, which can be very exhausting. In addition, emergency nurses are often on call in the event of a disaster, severe accident, or some other situation where additional staff may be needed.

Exploring

You can explore your interest in the nursing field in a number of ways. You can read books on careers in nursing and talk with high school guidance counselors, school nurses, and local public health nurses. Visit hospitals to observe the work and to talk with hospital personnel.

Some hospitals now have extensive volunteer service programs in which students can work after school, on weekends, or during vacations. You can find other volunteer work experiences with the Red Cross or community health services. Camp counseling jobs sometimes offer related experiences. Some schools offer participation in Future Nurses programs.

Employers

Nurses are employed by hospitals, managed-care facilities, long-term-care facilities, clinics, industry, private homes, schools, camps, and government agencies.

Starting Out

The only way to become a registered nurse is through completion of one of the three kinds of educational programs, plus passing the licensing examination. Registered nurses may apply for employment directly to hospitals, nursing homes, companies, and government agencies that hire nurses. Jobs can also be obtained through school placement offices, by signing up with employment agencies specializing in placement of nursing personnel, or through the state employment office. Other sources of jobs include nurses' associations, professional journals, and newspaper want ads.

Advancement

Administrative and supervisory positions in the nursing field go to nurses who have earned at least the bachelor of science degree in nursing. Nurses with many years of experience who are graduates of the diploma program may achieve supervisory positions, but requirements for such promotions have become more difficult in recent years and in many cases require at least the bachelor of science in nursing degree.

Earnings

According to the U.S. Department of Labor's *Occupational Outlook Handbook,* registered nurses earned an average of $40,690 annually in 1998. The low 10 percent earned less than $29,480, while the middle 50 percent earned between $34,430 and $49,070. The top 10 percent made over $69,300 a year. However, emergency nurses in certain areas may earn more.

Salary is determined by many factors, including nursing specialty, education, place of employment, shift worked, geographical location, and work experience. Flexible schedules and part-time employment opportunities are available for most nurses. Employers usually provide health and life insurance, and some offer educational reimbursements and year-end bonuses to their full-time staff.

Work Environment

Camps, government institutions, corporations, businesses, correctional institutions, and other health care environments may employ emergency nurses. Many emergency nurses work in hospital emergency rooms or emergency care centers. Most hospital and institutional environments are clean and well lighted. Inner city facilities and hospitals may be in less than desirable locations and safety may be an issue. Generally, emergency nurses who wish to advance in their careers will find themselves working in larger facilities in major cities.

All nursing careers have some health and disease risks; however, adherence to health and safety guidelines greatly minimizes the chance of contracting infectious diseases such as hepatitis and AIDS. Medical knowledge and good safety measures are also needed to limit the nurse's exposure to toxic chemicals, radiation, and other hazards.

Outlook

Nursing specialties will be in great demand in the future. The U.S. Bureau of Labor Statistics lists nursing as one of 10 occupations with the largest growth rate. From 1998 to 2008, jobs for registered nurses are expected to increase by 21.6 percent. The U.S. Bureau of Labor Statistics projects that employment for registered nurses will grow faster than the average for all occupations through 2008.

The unemployment rate for all nursing professions according to the American Association of Colleges of Nursing is less than 2 percent.

For More Information

American Association of Colleges of Nursing
One Dupont Circle, NW, Suite 530
Washington, DC 20036
Tel: 202-463-6930
Fax: 202-785-8320
Web: http://www.aacn.nche.edu/

Emergency Nurses Association
915 Lee Street
Des Plaines, IL 60016-6569
Tel: 800-900-9659
Fax: 847-460-4001
Web: http://www.ena.org

Geriatric Nurses

	School Subjects
Biology	
Chemistry	

	Personal Interests
Helping/teaching	
Technical/scientific	

	Work Environment
Primarily indoors	
Primarily one location	

	Minimum Education Level
Some postsecondary training	

	Salary Range
$30,000 to $50,000 to $80,000	

	Certification or Licensing
Required by all states	

	Outlook
Much faster than the average	

Overview

Geriatric nurses provide direct patient care to elderly people in their homes, or in hospitals, nursing homes, and clinics. The term "geriatrics" refers to the clinical aspects of aging and the overall health care of the aging population. Since older people tend to have different reactions to illness and disease than younger people, treating them has become a specialty, and because the population is aging, the geriatric nurse is a promising nursing specialty.

The Job

According to Jean Abdollahian, RN, NHA, a retired geriatric nurse and nursing home administrator, "Geriatric nursing is a different kind of nursing. These patients need a special kind of nursing and they almost always need more attention."

She continues, "In many aspects, geriatric nursing parallels pediatric nursing. Some elderly patients may have illnesses of child-like qualities that demand attention, love, and special medical care." Abdollahian adds, "The caregiver must have patience and a good sense of humor to deal with many trying situations."

Geriatric nurses focus primarily on caring for elderly patients. This care may be provided in an institution, in the home as a visiting nurse or hospice nurse, in a retirement community, in a doctor's office, in the hospital, or at wellness clinics in the community. Some geriatric nurses may also give health seminars or workshops to the elderly in the community, or they may be involved in research or pilot studies that deal with health and disease among the aging population.

Geriatric nurses can expect to perform many of the skills required of any nursing professional. And, many nurses who specialize in other types of care, with the exception of pediatrics and obstetrics, almost always find themselves caring for the elderly as well.

There are many nursing specialties under the broad umbrella of geriatric nursing. Abdollahian notes from her past experience, "A geriatrics nurse touches on almost all aspects of nursing; from intensive care, to emergency, to cardiac, to oncology. There are specialties within the specialty."

A common geriatrics specialty is a medications nurse who has additional pharmacology training. This nurse has an extensive knowledge of drugs, medication, and their effects on the elderly, in particular, and oversees the administration of medications to patients. Abdollahian notes that many state and federal laws now dictate how facilities can restrain their patients either physically or medicinally, so the medications nurse must be aware of these laws and see that the facility abides by these rules.

Another type of geriatric nurse is a charge nurse who oversees a particular shift of nurses and aides who care for the elderly. Although all health providers are required to do a lot of paperwork to document the care they provide and the patient's progress, the charge nurse and administrators are responsible for even more documentation required by HMOs, the federal government, and insurance providers.

Advancement into administration positions such as nursing home administrator or director of nursing is common for persons involved in a geriatric nursing career.

"This is a very rewarding area of nursing," says Abdollahian. "This is a fascinating age to work with. They have gone from the horse and buggy days to seeing a man walk on the moon. They have so many stories to tell."

Requirements

Postsecondary Training

Nurse practitioners who specialize in a specific nursing field must first become registered nurses. (See *Registered Nurses.*) Currently, there is no specific program for geriatric nursing in basic RN education; however, a few nursing school curriculums have elective courses in gerontology. Master's degree programs in gerontology are available at a few colleges. Nurses, who wish to focus on caring for elderly people may also choose to attend graduate school to become a nurse practitioner (See *Nurse Practitioners*) or clinical nurse specialist (See *Clinical Nurse Specialists*).

Certification or Licensing

Geriatric nursing certification is voluntary.

Other Requirements

Geriatric nurses should enjoy working with, and being around older people. They must have a general interest in aging and understand the problems related to growing older. The geriatric nurse must have the ability to get along with the patient's family members and must be able to work well with other professionals such as hospice nurses, chaplains, and social workers. Being able to work as part of a team is essential since many people may become involved in the health care and health needs of the elderly person. Communication skills are also essential. The nurse must be able to communicate with the family and the patient and explain medical terminology and procedures to them so they understand what is being done and why.

Exploring

You can explore your interest in the nursing field in a number of ways. You can read books on careers in nursing and talk with high school guidance counselors, school nurses, and local public health nurses. Visit hospitals to observe the work and to talk with hospital personnel.

Some hospitals now have extensive volunteer service programs in which students can work after school, on weekends, or during vacations. You can find other volunteer work experiences with the Red Cross or community health services. Camp counseling jobs sometimes offer related experiences. Some schools offer participation in Future Nurses programs.

Employers

Nurses are employed by hospitals, managed-care facilities, long-term-care facilities, clinics, industry, private homes, schools, camps, and government agencies.

Starting Out

The only way to become a registered nurse is through completion of one of the three kinds of educational programs, plus passing the licensing examination. Registered nurses may apply for employment directly to hospitals, nursing homes, companies, and government agencies that hire nurses. Jobs can also be obtained through school placement offices, by signing up with employment agencies specializing in placement of nursing personnel, or through the state employment office. Other sources of jobs include nurses' associations, professional journals, and newspaper want ads.

Advancement

Administrative and supervisory positions in the nursing field go to nurses who have earned at least the bachelor of science degree in nursing. Nurses with many years of experience who are graduates of the diploma program may achieve supervisory positions, but requirements for such promotions have become more difficult in recent years and in many cases require at least the bachelor of science in nursing degree.

Earnings

According to the U.S. Department of Labor's *Occupational Outlook Handbook,* registered nurses earned an average of $40,690 annually in 1998. The low 10 percent earned less than $29,480, while the middle 50 percent earned between $34,430 and $49,070. The top 10 percent made over $69,300 a year. However, geriatric specialty nurses can generally expect to earn more, especially when advancing to administrative positions.

Salary is determined by many factors, including nursing specialty, education, and place of employment, shift worked, geographical location, and work experience. Flexible schedules and part-time employment opportunities are available for most nurses. Employers usually provide health and life insurance, and some offer educational reimbursements and year-end bonuses to their full-time staff.

Work Environment

Geriatric nurses can expect to work in a variety of settings depending on their nursing responsibilities. Many geriatric nurses work in nursing homes, hospitals, retirement communities, or in clinics. They may also work with hospice and community nursing programs, or as office nurses for gerontologists.

Although most health care environments will be clean and well lighted, there may be some nursing situations where the surroundings may be less than desirable or where safety may be an issue.

All nursing careers have some health and disease risks; however, adherence to health and safety guidelines greatly minimizes the chance of contracting infectious diseases such as hepatitis and AIDS. Medical knowledge and good safety measures are also needed to limit the nurse's exposure to toxic chemicals, radiation, and other hazards.

Outlook

Nursing specialties will be in great demand in the future. The U.S. Bureau of Labor Statistics lists nursing as one of 10 occupations with the largest growth rate. From 1998 to 2008, jobs for registered nurses are expected to increase by 21.6 percent. In addition, the unemployment rate for all nursing professions reported by the American Association of Critical Care Nurses (AACN) is less than 2 percent.

Job opportunities for individuals who enter geriatric nursing will likely grow at a rate much faster than the average. The U.S. Bureau of the Census estimates that the number of individuals aged 65 or older will double by 2050. As the older population increases, their need for medical care will also increase. The need for nurses in nursing homes and home health care is expected to grow rapidly as citizens who are living into their 80s and 90s require extended health care.

For More Information

American Association of Colleges of Nursing
One Dupont Circle, NW, Suite 530
Washington, DC 20036
Tel: 202-463-6930
Web: http://www.aacn.nche.edu

American Geriatrics Society
350 Fifth Avenue, Suite 801
New York, NY 10118
Tel: 212-308-1414
Web: http://www.americangeriatrics.org

National Gerontological Nursing Association
7794 Grow Drive
Pensacola, FL 32514-7072
Tel: 850-473-1174

Home Health Care and Hospice Nurses

	School Subjects
Biology	
Chemistry	
	Personal Interests
Helping/teaching	
Technical/scientific	
	Work Environment
Primarily indoors	
Primarily multiple locations	
	Minimum Education Level
Some postsecondary training	
	Salary Range
$30,000 to $40,000 to $70,000	
	Certification or Licensing
Required by all states	
	Outlook
Faster than the average	

Overview

Home health care nurses provide home-based health care under the direction of a physician. They care for persons who may be recovering from an accident, illness, surgery, cancer, or childbirth. This type of home care originated with the Visiting Nurse Agencies (VNAs) more than 110 years ago. Today, as patients spend less time in the hospital and as more medical procedures are done on an outpatient basis, the need for professional follow-up care is essential. Visiting nurses care for nearly 10 million people every year. Home health care nurses may work for a community organization, a private health care provider, or they may be independent nurses who work on a contract basis.

While home health care nurses care for patients expecting to recover, *hospice nurses* care for people who are in the final stages of a terminal illness. Typically, a hospice patient has less than six months to live. Hospice nurses provide medical and emotional support to the patients and their families and friends. Hospice care usually takes place in the patient's home, but patients may also receive hospice care in a hospital room, nursing home, or a relative's home. The National Hospice and Palliative Care Organization states, "Hospice care professionals and volunteers provide services that address all of the symptoms of a terminal illness—ranging from physical to emotional to spiritual—with the aim of promoting comfort and dignity and living as fully as possible at life's end.

Both home health care and hospice nursing professions utilize a team approach in caring for their patients. Support people such as volunteers, aides, therapists, social workers, and clergy are often involved in the patient's care, as well as doctors. Hospice nurses usually work for a hospice or home care organization. The National Hospice Organization estimated that 540,000 patients were served by hospice or home care organizations in the United States in 1998.

The Job

Home health care nurses are often assigned to patients after the patients are discharged from a hospital or after they have had outpatient procedures. They provide follow-up health care on a regular basis and establish a one-on-one patient/nurse relationship. Some home health care nurses also work with patients who have acute, ongoing illnesses such as diabetes or high blood pressure.

According to Joan Bissing, RN, BS, a hospice nurse in California, "We [home health care and hospice nurses] often provide wound care, draw blood, and give medications. We may also do chemotherapy, or IV therapy.

"It is essential that a hospice or home health care nurse have nursing experience before going into this specialty," Bissing states. "While most nurses work directly under a doctor, hospice and home health care nurses must have a specialty in high-tech nursing and a knowledge of different diseases since they are often required to work independently."

Although they need to be able to work alone, this nursing specialty must also know how to work as a team. A variety of hospice personnel such as doctors, social workers, chaplains, volunteers, counselors, and aides become involved with the patient as the illness progresses. Home health care and hospice nurses work with all aspects and ages of the population. Their duties vary greatly depending on their patients, their illness, and the care or support they need.

Sometimes the job requires the nurse to "just listen," says Bissing. "We can sometimes sense that our terminally ill patient is unsettled about something, such as past relationships, and then we need to be proactive and get the proper counseling or clergy to help the patient deal with the problem and find peace."

The hospice nurse is often a source of comfort to the patient and their family and friends. "Some patients may say, I've had enough treatments. I just want to live my final days as peacefully and pain-free as possible," Bissing says. The hospice nurse must work with the hospice team to make sure those wishes are carried out. "At that point, we focus on giving the patient the best quality of life we can, keeping the patient as comfortable and pain-free as possible."

There are rewards to every member of the hospice team, according to Bissing. "They all learn something from each of their patients. Sometimes it is an experience they won't ever forget." She goes on, "It can be as simple as a touch of the hand with a difficult patient, or as complex as facilitating a reunion with a long-lost relative before the patient's death."

One thing Bissing wants anyone thinking of going into this profession to remember, "Never forget that it's okay to cry. Shared tears are often part of the patient care."

Requirements

Postsecondary Training

Nurses who specialize in a specific nursing field such as home health care or hospice nursing must first become registered nurses. (See *Registered Nurses.*) Many home health care and hospice nurses are required to have some nursing experience, preferably in acute care, since they are required to work with patients with a wide range of health problems. Entry-level requirements depend on the home health care agency, the hospice organization, and the availability of nurses in that specialty and geographical region. Certification is a voluntary process. Nurses who wish to specialize in hospice or home health care may choose to attend graduate school.

Other Requirements

As with almost all health care professions today, nurses spend a great deal of time keeping records and charts, and documenting the services they provide in order to meet insurance, government, and Medicare requirements.

Home health care and hospice nurses should feel comfortable working with patients of all ages and people from all cultural backgrounds. Good communication skills are essential, including the ability to listen and respond to the patients' needs. Home health care and hospice nurses must be able to work independently, have good organizational skills, and also have the ability to supervise aides and other support people. Flexibility is also a requirement since duties vary greatly from hour to hour and day to day. Many hospice nurses are on call and their work is mentally stressful. "There is a lot of burnout in hospice nursing," confirms Bissing. "Hospice nurses usually don't stay in the field long. It is hard work and very intense. Much of hospice nursing is treating the symptoms of the disease, rather than curing the disease."

Exploring

You can explore your interest in the nursing field in a number of ways. You can read books on careers in nursing and talk with high school guidance counselors, school nurses, and local public health nurses. Visit hospitals to observe the work and to talk with hospital personnel.

Some hospitals now have extensive volunteer service programs in which students can work after school, on weekends, or during vacations. You can find other volunteer work experiences with the Red Cross or community health services. Camp counseling jobs sometimes offer related experiences. Some schools offer participation in Future Nurses programs.

Employers

Nurses are employed by hospitals, managed-care facilities, long-term-care facilities, clinics, industry, private homes, schools, camps, and government agencies.

Starting Out

The only way to become a registered nurse is through completion of one of the three kinds of educational programs, plus passing the licensing examination. Registered nurses may apply for employment directly to hospitals, nursing homes, companies, and government agencies that hire nurses. Jobs can also be obtained through school placement offices, by signing up with employment agencies specializing in placement of nursing personnel, or through the state employment office. Other sources of jobs include nurses' associations, professional journals, and newspaper want ads.

Advancement

Administrative and supervisory positions in the nursing field go to nurses who have earned at least the bachelor of science degree in nursing. Nurses with many years of experience who are graduates of the diploma program may achieve supervisory positions, but requirements for such promotions have become more difficult in recent years and in many cases require at least the bachelor of science in nursing degree.

Earnings

According to the U.S. Department of Labor's *Occupational Outlook Handbook*, registered nurses earned an average of $40,690 annually in 1998. The low 10 percent earned less than $29,480, while the middle 50 percent earned between $34,430 and $49,070. The top 10 percent made over $69,300 a year.

Salary is determined by many factors, including nursing specialty, education, place of employment, geographical location, and work experience. Flexible schedules are available for most full-time nurses and part-time work is often available. Employers usually provide health and life insurance, and some offer educational reimbursements and year-end bonuses to their full-time staff.

Work Environment

Most hospice and home health care nurses care for their patients in the patients' homes, nursing homes, or in the homes of their caregivers, so the work environment can be as varied as their patients' lifestyles. In addition, patients and family members can be very tense during this stressful period of their lives and they may be unpleasant and uncooperative at times. Some nurses are on call 24 hours a day and may be required to travel to homes in all neighborhoods of a city or in remote rural areas day and night. Safety may be an issue at times.

All nursing careers have some health and disease risks; however, adherence to health and safety guidelines greatly minimizes the chance of contracting infectious diseases such as hepatitis and AIDS. Medical knowledge and good safety measures are also needed to limit the nurse's exposure to toxic chemicals, radiation, and other hazards.

Outlook

Nursing specialties will be in great demand in the future. The U.S. Bureau of Labor Statistics lists nursing as one of 10 occupations with the largest growth rate. From 1998 to 2008, jobs in nursing are expected to increase by 21.6 percent. In addition, the unemployment rate for all nursing professions reported by the American Association of Critical Care Nurses (AACN) is less than 2 percent. Part-time job opportunities are also plentiful in the nursing profession.

The nursing demand will be felt particularly in the hospice and home health care fields. The U.S. Bureau of the Census estimates that the number of individuals aged 65 or older will double by 2050. As the older population increases, their need for medical care will also increase. Hospice participation has grown at a dramatic rate, especially among those involved with Medicare. This number is expected to increase as the population ages and health care costs rise.

For More Information

American Association of Colleges of Nursing
One Dupont Circle, Suite 530
Washington, DC   20036
Tel: 202-463-6930
Web: http://www.aacn.nche.edu/

National Association for Home Care
228 Seventh Street, SE
Washington, DC 20003-4306
Tel: 202-547-7424
Web: http://www.nahc.org

National Hospice and Palliative Care Organization
1700 Diagonal Road, Suite 300
Alexandria, VA 22314
Tel: 800-658-8898
Web: http://www.nhpco.org

Visiting Nurse Associations of America
11 Beacon Street, Suite 910
Boston, MA 02108
Tel: 617-523-4042
Web: http://www.vnaa.org

Legal Nurse Consultants

	School Subjects
Biology Chemistry	
	Personal Interests
Helping/teaching Technical/scientific	
	Work Environment
Primarily indoors Primarily multiple locations	
	Minimum Education Level
Some postsecondary training	
	Salary Range
$25,000 to $45,000 to $100,000	
	Certification or Licensing
Required by all states	
	Outlook
Faster than the average	

Overview

Legal nurse consultants are members of a litigation team that deals with medical malpractice, personal injury, and product liability lawsuits as well as other medically related legal cases. They may be employed independently on a contract or retainer basis; or they may be employed by a law firm, insurance company, corporation, government agency, or as part of a risk management department in a hospital. Legal nurse consultants are trained nurses who have a thorough understanding of medical issues and trends. They utilize their clinical experience, knowledge of health care standards, and medical resources to assist litigation teams and act as liaisons between the legal and health care communities. Their primary role is to evaluate, analyze, and render informed opinions regarding health care. They practice in both plaintiff and defense capacities in collaboration with attorneys and others involved in legal processes.

The Job

Legal nurse consultants' job responsibilities vary depending on the case and its medical implications. When working on a case, they may conduct client interviews, which involves talking to persons who feel they have a legal claim against a medical facility or doctor or nurse, or as a result of an accident.

They may research past medical cases and treatments. They often advise attorneys regarding medical facts, treatments, and other medical issues that are relevant to a case. Legal nurse consultants obtain and organize medical records, and locate and procure evidence. They may identify, interview, and retain expert witnesses. They may also assist with depositions and trials, including developing and preparing exhibits for jury or judge trials.

As part of legal teams, legal nurse consultants are often required to do considerable research and paperwork. "As a legal nurse consultant," says Sherri Reed, BSN, RN, LNCC, and president of the American Association of Legal Nurse Consultants (AALNC), "you must be totally responsible for your part of the job. If information is to be gathered and reports written, you need to get it done. There is no one to take over at shift change. It is entirely your responsibility and you can't pass it on to someone else."

Independent legal nurse consultants must also be responsible for getting their work done within a strict deadline. They often work under a contract and must produce the records, information, and reports within a specified time frame.

In addition, they must generate their own clients. This requires that they not only be nurses, but be businesspersons as well and do their own marketing to the legal field. Independent legal nurse consultants need to learn and practice business skills such as marketing, sales, and record keeping.

"Nurses are nurturers by nature," says Reed. "Because of these predominant traits, many need to learn to be aggressive and assertive and be their own salespeople if they are going to find work."

Legal nurse consultants can expect their jobs to be demanding, but that is what Reed likes best about her job. "I like my independence and using my knowledge to analyze and research cases. It is challenging and stimulating. There are always new cases and issues."

Requirements

Postsecondary Training

Nurse practitioners who specialize in a specific nursing field such as legal nurse consultants must first become registered nurses. (See *Registered Nurses.*) "All legal nurse consultants must have clinical nursing experience," says Reed who is employed as a legal nurse consultant with an Indiana law firm. "This is extremely important since they need this work experience to draw on in order to present cases and testify. They must have up-to-date medical knowledge they can utilize."

Legal nurse consultants should have work experience in critical care areas such as hospital emergency rooms, intensive care units, and obstetrics, since these are the areas that are most likely to be involved in litigation. Legal education is not a prerequisite, although many legal nurse consultants acquire knowledge of the legal system by consulting with attorneys, taking classes, and attending seminars.

Many independent legal nurse consultants are practicing nurses. According to Reed, "It is important for legal nurse consultants to stay abreast of changes in the medical field. They need to actively practice nursing or take continuing education courses to stay current. They must be able to apply their knowledge and evaluate medical issues in litigation."

Certification or Licensing

A legal nurse consultant certificate (LNCC) is voluntary and is accredited by the American Board of Nursing Specialties. This credential demonstrates that the legal nurse consultant has met practice experience requirements and has passed an examination testing all areas of legal nurse consulting. The certificate is renewed every five years through continuing education or re-examination and continued practice in the specialty.

Exploring

You can explore your interest in the nursing field in a number of ways. You can read books on careers in nursing and talk with high school guidance counselors, school nurses, and local public health nurses. Visit hospitals to observe the work and to talk with hospital personnel.

Some hospitals now have extensive volunteer service programs in which students can work after school, on weekends, or during vacations. You can find other volunteer work experiences with the Red Cross or community health services. Camp counseling jobs sometimes offer related experiences. Some schools offer participation in Future Nurses programs.

Employers

Nurses are employed by hospitals, managed-care facilities, long-term-care facilities, clinics, industry, private homes, schools, camps, and government agencies.

Starting Out

The only way to become a registered nurse is through completion of one of the three kinds of educational programs, plus passing the licensing examination. Registered nurses may apply for employment directly to hospitals, nursing homes, companies, and government agencies that hire nurses. Jobs can also be obtained through school placement offices, by signing up with employment agencies specializing in placement of nursing personnel, or through the state employment office. Other sources of jobs include nurses' associations, professional journals, and newspaper want ads.

Advancement

Administrative and supervisory positions in the nursing field go to nurses who have earned at least the bachelor of science degree in nursing. Nurses with many years of experience who are graduates of the diploma program may achieve supervisory positions, but requirements for such promotions have become more difficult in recent years and in many cases require at least the bachelor of science in nursing degree.

Earnings

Persons who work as independent legal nurse consultants are usually paid on an hourly basis that can range from $50 to $125 per hour. The fee depends on the type of services they are performing, such as testifying, reviewing records, or doing medical research, and also reflects their experience and reputation. In addition, fees vary in different parts of the country. Some legal nurse consultants may work on a retainer basis with one or more clients.

Many legal nurse consultants who work for law firms and other businesses and institutions are employed full- or part-time. Their salaries vary by experience, geographic location, and areas of expertise. The full-time salary range is from under $30,000 to a small percentage making over $100,000. Some litigation situations may require that consultants work overtime.

General employment benefits such as health and life insurance, vacation time, and sick leave may be offered to full-time legal nurse consultants.

Work Environment

Working environments may vary depending on the consultants' responsibilities and their legal cases. According to a survey conducted by AALNC, 53 percent of legal nurse consultants were in independent practice, and 32 percent were employed by law firms. Office environments where consultants work are usually clean and well lighted. However, research and interview requirements may take consultants to communities that range from safe to less than desirable.

Outlook

Nursing specialties will be in great demand in the future. The U.S. Bureau of Labor Statistics lists nursing as one of 10 occupations with the largest growth rate. From 1998 to 2008, jobs in nursing are expected to increase by 21.6 percent.

The outlook for legal nurse consultants is excellent. According to Reed, "It is an up-and-coming profession. Our association [AALNC] has grown rapidly and we hope to increase the profession's visibility."

For More Information

American Association of Colleges of Nursing
One Dupont Circle, NW, Suite 530
Washington, DC 20036
Tel: 202-463-6930
Web: http://www.aacn.nche.edu

American Association of Legal Nurse Consultants
4700 West Lake Avenue
Glenview, IL 60025-1485
Tel: 877-402-2562
Web: http://www.aalnc.org

Licensed Practical Nurses

School Subjects
- Biology
- Chemistry

Personal Skills
- Helping/teaching
- Technical/scientific

Work Environment
- Primarily indoors
- Primarily multiple locations

Minimum Education Level
- Some postsecondary training

Salary Range
- $20,000 to $27,000 to $37,500

Certification or Licensing
- Required by all states

Outlook
- About as fast as the average

Overview

Licensed practical nurses (LPNs), a specialty of the nursing profession, are sometimes called licensed vocational nurses. LPNs are trained to assist in the care and treatment of patients. They may assist registered nurses and physicians or work under various other circumstances. They perform many of the general duties of nursing and may be responsible for some clerical duties. LPNs work in hospitals, public health agencies, nursing homes, or in home health.

The Job

Licensed practical nurses work under the supervision of a registered nurse, or a physician. They are responsible for many general duties of nursing such as administering prescribed drugs and medical treatments to patients, taking patients' temperatures and blood pressures, assisting in the preparation of medical examination and surgery, and performing routine laboratory tests. LPNs help with therapeutic and rehabilitation sessions; they may also participate in the planning, practice, and evaluation of a patient's nursing care.

A primary duty of an LPN is to ensure that patients are clean and comfortable, and that their needs, both physical and emotional, are met. They sometimes assist patients with daily hygiene such as bathing, brushing teeth, and dressing. Many times they provide emotional comfort by simply talking with the patient.

LPNs working in nursing homes have duties similar to those employed by hospitals. They provide bedside care, administer medications, develop care plans, and supervise nurse assistants. Those working in doctors' offices and clinics are sometimes required to perform clerical duties such as keeping records, maintaining files and paperwork, as well as answering phones and tending the appointment book. Home health LPNs, in addition to their nursing duties, may sometimes prepare and serve meals to their patients.

Requirements

High School

Some LPN programs do not require a high school diploma, but it is highly recommended, particularly if you want to consider advancement opportunities. To prepare for a career as an LPN, students should study biology, chemistry, physics, and science while in high school. English and mathematics courses are also helpful.

Postsecondary Training

Those interested in a career as an LPN usually enroll in a practical nursing program after graduating from high school. There were about 1,100 state approved programs in the United States in 1997 providing practical nursing training. According to the U.S. Department of Labor, 60 percent of all LPNs graduate from a technical or vocational school and 30 percent from a community or junior college. The remainder were enrolled in colleges, hospital programs, or high schools. Most programs last from 12 to 18 months, with time spent for both classroom study and supervised clinical care. Courses include basic nursing concepts, anatomy, physiology, medical-surgical nursing, pediatrics, obstetrics, nutrition, and first aid. Clinical practice is most often in a hospital setting.

Certification or Licensing

All 50 states require graduates of a state-approved practical nursing program to take a licensing examination. LPNs may also take the Certification Exam for Practical and Vocational Nurses in Long-Term Care (CEPN-LTC). Contact the National Council of State Boards of Nursing, Inc., for more information.

Other Requirements

Stamina, both physical and mental, is a must for this occupation. LPNs may be assigned to care for heavy or immobile patients or patients confused with dementia. Patience, and a caring, nurturing attitude, are valuable qualities to possess in order to be a successful LPN. As part of a health care team, they must be able to follow orders and work under close supervision.

Exploring

High school students can explore an interest in this career by reading books or by checking out Web sites devoted to the nursing field. You should also take advantage of any information available in your school career center. An excellent way to learn more about this career first hand is to speak with the school nurse or local public health nurse. Visits to the local hospital can give you a feel for the work environment. Volunteer work at a hospital, community health center, or even the local Red Cross chapter can provide valuable experience. Some high schools offer membership in Future Nurses organizations.

Employers

LPNs are employed at hospitals, clinics, doctors' offices, nursing homes, home health care agencies, and public health agencies.

Starting Out

After licensing requirements are fulfilled, LPNs should check with human resource departments of hospitals, nursing homes, and clinics for openings. Employment agencies that specialize in health professions, and state employment agencies are other ways to find employment, as are school placement centers. Newspaper classified ads, nurses associations, and professional journals are great sources of job opportunities.

Advancement

About 40 percent of LPNs use their license and experience as a stepping stone for other occupations in the health field, many of which offer more responsibility and higher salaries. Some LPNs, for example, with additional training, become medical technicians, surgical attendants, optometric assistants, or psychiatric technicians. Many LPNs return to school to become registered nurses. Hospitals often offer LPNs the opportunity for more training, seminars, workshops, and clinical sessions to sharpen their nursing skills.

Earnings

According to the *Occupational Outlook Handbook,* LPNs earned an average of $26,940 annually in 1998. 50 percent earned between $23,160 and $31,870; the top 10 percent earned over $37,540. A recent Buck Survey listed average earnings for LPNs employed at national chain nursing homes in 1996 at $12 an hour, or $480 weekly. Many LPNs are able to supplement their salaries with overtime pay and shift differentials. One-third of all LPNs work part-time.

Work Environment

Most LPNs work 40-hour weeks, less if part-time. As with other health professionals, they may be asked to work during nights, weekends, or holidays to provide 24-hour care for their patients. Nurses are usually given pay differentials for these shifts.

LPNs employed in hospitals and nursing homes, as well as in clinics, enjoy clean, well lighted, and generally comfortable work environments. The nature of their work calls for LPNs to be on their feet for most of the shift—providing patient care, dispensing medication, or assisting other health personnel.

Outlook

There were about 692,000 LPNs employed in the United States in 1998. Thirty-two percent worked in hospitals; 28 percent were employed in nursing homes; and 14 percent treated patients in doctors' offices and clinics. The remainder of LPNs worked for home health or temporary agencies.

Employment prospects for LPNs are expected to grow about as fast as the average for all occupations through 2008. Opportunities in nursing homes are expected to grow faster than the average. A growing elderly population requiring long-term health care is the primary factor for the demand of qualified LPNs. Traditionally, hospitals provide the most job opportunities for LPNs. However, this source will only provide a moderate number of openings in the future. Inpatient population is not expected to increase significantly. Also, in many hospitals, certified nursing attendants (See *Nurse Assistants*) are increasingly taking over many of the duties of LPNs.

Demand for LPNs will be greatest in nursing home settings and home health care agencies. Due to advanced medical technology, people are able to live longer, though many will require medical assistance. Private medical practices will also be good job sources because many medical procedures are now being performed on an outpatient basis in doctors' offices.

For More Information

The following organizations have information on education programs and careers.

American Association of Colleges of Nursing
1 Dupont Circle, Suite 530
Washington, DC 20036
Tel: 202-463-6930
Web: http://www.aacn.nche.edu

National Association for Practical Nurse Education and Service, Inc.
1400 Spring Street, Suite 330
Silver Spring, MD 20910
Tel: 301-588-2491
Email: napnes@aol.com

For information on certification, contact:

National Council of State Boards of Nursing, Inc.
676 N. St. Clair Street, Suite 550
Chicago, IL 60611-2921
Tel: 312-787-6555
Web: http://www.ncsbn.org

For career information, contact:

National Federation of Licensed Practical Nurses, Inc.
893 US Highway 70 West, Suite 202
Garner, NC 27529
Tel: 919-779-0046
Web: http://www.nflpn.org/

For information about careers, employment opportunities, and certification, contact:

National League for Nursing
Communications Department
350 Hudson Street
New York, NY 10014
Tel: 212-989-9393
Email: nlnweb@nln.org
Web: http://www.nln.org

Neonatal Nurses

	School Subjects
Biology Chemistry	

	Personal Interests
Helping/teaching Technical/scientific	

	Work Environment
Primarily indoors Primarily one location	

	Minimum Education Level
Some postsecondary training	

	Salary Range
$30,000 to $50,000 to $75,000	

	Certification or Licensing
Required by all states	

	Outlook
Faster than the average	

Overview

Neonatal nurses provide direct patient care to newborns in hospitals. The babies they care for may be normal babies, or they may be born prematurely, or the newborns may be suffering from an illness or birth defect. Some of the babies require highly technical care such as surgery, or the use of ventilators, incubators, or intravenous feedings.

The Job

Neonatal nurses care for newborn babies in hospitals. Depending on the size of the hospital, their duties may vary. Some neonatal nurses may be in the delivery room and, as soon as the baby is born, are responsible for cleaning up the baby, visually assessing it, and drawing blood by pricking the newborn's heel. This blood sample is sent to the laboratory where a number of screening tests are performed as required by the state. These assessments help the staff and doctor determine if the baby is normal or needs additional testing, a special diet, or intensive care. Sharon Stout, RN, who was a neonatal nurse for six years in Georgia, said she loved being in the delivery room and caring for the newborn because she enjoyed seeing the interaction with the baby and the new mother and family. "It was usually a very happy time."

"However," she says, "if a baby needed special care that we could not provide at our facility, we stabilized it until the neonatal transport team arrived from a larger hospital to transfer the baby to its special neonatal care unit."

Babies who are born without complications are usually placed in a Level I nursery or in the mother's room with her. However, because of today's short hospital stays for mother and child, many hospitals no longer have Level I, or healthy baby nurseries. Neonatal or general staff nurses help the new mothers care for their newborns in their hospital rooms.

Level II is a special care nursery for babies who have been born prematurely or who may have an illness, disease, or birth defect. These babies are also cared for by a neonatal nurse, or a staff nurse with more advanced training in caring for newborns. These babies may need oxygen, intravenous therapies, special feedings, or because of underdevelopment, may simply need more time to mature.

Specialized neonatal nurses or more advanced degree nurses care for babies placed in the Level III neonatal intensive care unit. This unit admits all babies who cannot be treated in either of the other two nurseries. These at-risk babies require high-tech care such as ventilators, incubators, or surgery. Level III units are generally found in larger hospitals or may be part of a children's hospital.

Requirements

Postsecondary Training

Neonatal nurses must be registered nurses. (See *Registered Nurses.*) There is no special program for neonatal nursing in basic RN education; however, some nursing programs have an elective course in neonatal nursing. Entry-level requirements to become a neonatal nurse depend on the institution, its size, and the availability of nurses in that specialty and geographical region. Some institutions may require neonatal nurses to demonstrate their ability in administering medications, performing necessary math calculations, suctioning, cardiopulmonary resuscitation, ventilator care, and other newborn care skills. Nurses who wish to focus on caring for premature babies or sick newborns may choose to attend graduate school to become a neonatal nurse practitioner or clinical nurse specialist.

Other Requirements

Neonatal nurses should like working with mothers, newborns, and families. This is a very intense nursing field, especially when caring for the high-risk infant, so the neonatal nurse should be compassionate, patient, and be able to handle stress and make decisions. The nurse should also be able to communicate well with other medical staff and the patients' families. Families of an at-risk newborn are often frightened and very worried about their infant. Because of their fears, family members may be difficult to deal with and the nurse must display patience, understanding, and composure during these emotional times. The nurse must be able to communicate with the family and explain medical terminology and procedures to them so they understand what is being done for their baby and why.

Exploring

You can explore your interest in the nursing field in a number of ways. You can read books on careers in nursing and talk with high school guidance counselors, school nurses, and local public health nurses. Visit hospitals to observe the work and to talk with hospital personnel.

Some hospitals now have extensive volunteer service programs in which students can work after school, on weekends, or during vacations. You can find other volunteer work experiences with the Red Cross or community health services. Camp counseling jobs sometimes offer related experiences. Some schools offer participation in Future Nurses programs.

Employers

Nurses are employed by hospitals, managed-care facilities, long-term-care facilities, clinics, industry, private homes, schools, camps, and government agencies.

Starting Out

The only way to become a registered nurse is through completion of one of the three kinds of educational programs, plus passing the licensing examination. Registered nurses may apply for employment directly to hospitals, nursing homes, companies, and government agencies that hire nurses. Jobs can also be obtained through school placement offices, by signing up with employment agencies specializing in placement of nursing personnel, or through the state employment office. Other sources of jobs include nurses' associations, professional journals, and newspaper want ads.

Advancement

Administrative and supervisory positions in the nursing field go to nurses who have earned at least the bachelor of science degree in nursing. Nurses with many years of experience who are graduates of the diploma program may achieve supervisory positions, but requirements for such promotions have become more difficult in recent years and in many cases require at least the bachelor of science in nursing degree.

Earnings

According to the U.S. Department of Labor's *Occupational Outlook Handbook*, registered nurses earned an average of $40,690 annually in 1998. The low 10 percent earned less than $29,480, while the middle 50 percent earned between $34,430 and $49,070. The top 10 percent made over $69,300 a year. However, neonatal specialty nurses can generally expect to earn more, especially when advancing to administrative positions. According to the National Association of Neonatal Nurses, the median salary is around $50,000 a year.

Salary is determined by many factors, including nursing specialty, education, and place of employment, shift worked, geographical location, and work experience. Flexible schedules and part-time employment opportunities are available for most nurses. Employers usually provide health and life insurance, and some offer educational reimbursements and year-end bonuses to their full-time staff.

Work Environment

Neonatal nurses can expect to work in a hospital environment that is clean and well lighted. Inner city hospitals may be in a less than desirable location and safety may be an issue. Generally, neonatal nurses who wish to advance in their careers will find themselves working in larger hospitals in major cities.

Nurses usually spend much of the day on their feet, either walking or standing. Many hospital nurses work 10- or 12-hour shifts, which can be tiring. Long hours and intense nursing demands can create burnout for some nurses, meaning that they often become dissatisfied with their jobs. Fortunately, there are many areas in which nurses can use their skills, so sometimes trying a different type of nursing may be the answer.

Outlook

Nursing specialties will be in great demand in the future. The U.S. Bureau of Labor Statistics lists nursing as one of 10 occupations with the largest growth rate. From 1998 to 2008, jobs in nursing are expected to increase by 21.6 percent.

The outlook for neonatal nurses is good, especially for those with master's degrees or higher. According to the National Association of Neonatal Nurses, positions should be available due to downsizing in previous years. These cutbacks have led to a decrease in the number of nurses choosing advanced practice education. Also, the average neonatal nurse today is middle-aged and may be moving on to less stressful areas of nursing.

For More Information

American Association of Colleges of Nursing
One Dupont Circle, NW, Suite 530
Washington, DC 20036
Tel: 202-463-6930
Web: http://www.aacn.nche.edu

National Association of Neonatal Nurses
701 Lee Street, Suite 450
Des Plaines, IL 60016
Tel: 847-299-6266
Web: http://www.nann.org/

Nurse Anesthetists

Biology Chemistry	School Subjects
Helping/teaching Technical/scientific	Personal Skills
Primarily indoors Primarily multiple locations	Work Environment
Master's degree	Minimum Education Level
$70,000 to $80,000 to $100,000+	Salary Range
Required by all states	Certification
Faster than the average	Outlook

Overview

Nurse anesthetists, also known as *certified registered nurse anesthetists* (CRNAs), are one of four classifications of *advanced practice nurses* (APNs). They are *registered nurses* (RNs) with advanced training in anesthesiology. They are responsible for administering, supervising, and monitoring anesthesia-related care for patients undergoing surgical procedures. General anesthesia is not necessary for all surgical procedures; therefore, nurse anesthetists also work on cases in which they provide various types of local anesthesia—topical, infiltration, nerve-block, spinal, and epidural or caudal. There are currently more than 30,000 nurse anesthetists working in the United States.

History

Reliable methods of putting a patient to sleep were first developed in the 1840s when the discovery of ether anesthesia revolutionized surgery. Before that time, when surgery offered the only possible chance of saving a person's life, all that the surgeon could do was give alcohol or opium to deaden the pain. Similarly, mandrake, hemp, and herbane may have been given orally, or by inhalation, during childbirth.

The first nurse anesthetist was Sister Mary Bernard, who practiced in Pennsylvania in the 1870s. The first school of nurse anesthetists was founded in 1909 at St. Vincent Hospital in Portland, Oregon. Since then, many schools have been established, and the nurse anesthesia specialty was formally created on June 17, 1931, when the American Association of Nurse Anesthetists (AANA) held its first meeting.

Contemporary anesthesiology is far more complicated and much more effective than in the early days when an ether- or chloroform-soaked cloth or sponge was held up to the patient's face. Today, a combination of several modern-day anesthetic agents is usually used to anesthetize the patient.

The Job

Approximately 26 million anesthetic procedures are carried out annually in U.S. medical facilities and 65 percent of these are administered by nurse anesthetists. In 70 percent of rural hospitals, nurse anesthetists are the only anesthesia providers.

Prior to surgery, a nurse anesthetist takes the patient's history, evaluates his or her anesthesia needs, and forms a plan for the best possible management of the case (often in consultation with an anesthesiologist). The nurse anesthetist also explains the planned procedures to the patient and answers questions the patient might have.

Prior to the operation, the nurse anesthetist administers an intravenous (IV) sedative to relax the patient. Then the nurse anesthetist administers a combination of drugs to establish and maintain the patient in a controlled state of unconsciousness, insensibility to pain, and muscular relaxation. Some general anesthetics are administered by inhalation through a mask and tube and others are administered intravenously. Because the muscular relaxants prevent patients from breathing on their own, the nurse anesthetist has to provide artificial respiration through a tube inserted into the windpipe.

Throughout the surgery, the nurse anesthetist monitors the patient's vital signs by watching the video and digital displays. The nurse anesthetist is also responsible for maintaining the patient's blood, water, and salt levels as well as continually readjusting the flow of anesthetics and other medications to ensure optimal results.

After surgery, nurse anesthetists monitor the patient's return to consciousness and watch for complications. The nurse anesthetists must be skilled in the use of airways, ventilators, IVs, blood- and fluid-replacement techniques, and postoperative pain management.

Requirements

Postsecondary Training

All applicants to nurse anesthetist programs must be registered nurses (See *Registered Nurses*), have a bachelor's degree, and at least one year's acute care nursing experience. There are over 90 accredited nurse anesthesia programs in the United States and the admissions process is competitive. The programs last 24 to 36 months and nearly all offer a master's degree. There are also a few clinical nursing doctorate programs for nurse anesthetists. Students take extensive classes in pharmacology and the sciences. They also acquire hundreds of hours of anesthesia-related clinical experience in surgery and obstetrics.

Certification or Licensing

Nurse anesthetists are required to pass a national certification exam after completing their educational program. All states recognize certified registered nurse anesthetist (CRNA) status. Certified nurse anesthetists are not required to work under the supervision of an anesthesiologist, although some licensing laws do stipulate that they must work with a physician.

CRNAs must be recertified every two years according to the criteria established by the Council on Recertification of the American Association of Nurse Anesthetists. Part of this requirement includes earning 40 continuing education credits every two years.

Other Requirements

Nurse anesthetists must have the ability to concentrate for long periods of time and remain focused on monitoring their patient during surgery. They must be able to analyze problems accurately and swiftly, make decisions quickly, and react appropriately. They must have the ability to remain calm during emergencies and be able to handle stressful situations.

Nurse anesthetists also need to have efficient time management skills in order to work efficiently with surgeons and their operating schedules.

Exploring

You can explore your interest in the nursing field in a number of ways. You can read books on careers in nursing and talk with high school guidance counselors, school nurses, and local public health nurses. Visit hospitals to observe the work and to talk with hospital personnel.

Some hospitals now have extensive volunteer service programs in which students can work after school, on weekends, or during vacations. You can find other volunteer work experiences with the Red Cross or community health services. Camp counseling jobs sometimes offer related experiences. Some schools offer participation in Future Nurses programs.

Employers

Nurses are employed by hospitals, managed-care facilities, long-term-care facilities, clinics, industry, private homes, schools, camps, and government agencies.

Starting Out

The only way to become a registered nurse is through completion of one of the three kinds of educational programs, plus passing the licensing examination. Registered nurses may apply for employment directly to hospitals, nursing homes, companies, and government agencies that hire nurses. Jobs can also be obtained through school placement offices, by signing up with employment agencies specializing in placement of nursing personnel, or through the state employment office. Other sources of jobs include nurses' associations, professional journals, and newspaper want ads.

Advancement

Administrative and supervisory positions in the nursing field go to nurses who have earned at least the bachelor of science degree in nursing. Nurses with many years of experience who are graduates of the diploma program may achieve supervisory positions, but requirements for such promotions have become more difficult in recent years and in many cases require at least the bachelor of science in nursing degree.

Employers

Many nurse anesthetists are employed by hospitals or outpatient surgery centers. Dentists and podiatrists, as well as same-day surgery centers, also employ them. Others may be employed in a group or independent practice that provides services to hospitals and other health care centers on a contract basis. Some work for rural hospitals, the U.S. Public Health Services, and the U.S. military. Because the high quality, cost-effective anesthesia service provided by nurse anesthetists is widely acknowledged, health care institutions are eager to employ them.

Earnings

Nurse anesthetists are one of the highest paid nursing specialists. Their salaries range from the $70,000s, to the $80,000s, to over $100,000 for experienced nurse anesthetists. The average annual salary reported by the American Association of Nurse Anesthetists in 1997 was approximately $87,000.

Fringe benefits are usually similar to other full-time health care workers and may include sick leave, vacation, health and life insurance, and tuition assistance.

Work Environment

Nurse anesthetists usually work in sterile, well-lighted operating facilities. They spend considerable time on their feet and may be required to stand for many hours at a time. Emergencies can produce a stressful and fast-paced environment. Many nurse anesthetists must be on call, usually on a rotation basis, to respond to emergency surgical situations.

Outlook

The American Association of Nurse Anesthetists (AANA) estimates that CRNAs administer approximately 65 percent of the 26 million anesthetics given to patients in the United States each year.

"The future looks bright for CRNAs," according to 1999 AANA President Linda R. Williams, CRNA, JD. "CRNAs are a glowing example of how advanced practice nurses can be used to provide affordable, high-quality health care to the citizens of this country." There is currently a shortage of CRNAs in the marketplace. With the current trend of cutting costs in all health care facilities, CRNAs provide an alternative to hiring high-priced anesthesiologists. The increased use of managed health care services and the aging population will also result in a need for additional nurse anesthetists.

For More Information

To learn more about a career as a nurse anesthetist, contact:

American Association of Nurse Anesthetists
222 South Prospect Avenue
Park Ridge, IL 60068-4001
Tel: 847-692-7050
Email: info@aana.com
Web: http://www.aana.com

American Society of PeriAnesthesia Nurses
6900 Grove Road
Thorofare, NY 08086
Tel: 609-845-5557
Email: aspan@slackinc.com
Web: http://www.aspan.org/

National League for Nursing
61 Broadway
New York, NY 10006
Tel: 212-363-5555
Email: nlnweb@nln.org
Web: http://www.nln.org

Nurse Assistants

Biology Health	School Subjects
Following instructions Helping/teaching	Personal Skills
Primarily indoors Primarily multiple locations	Work Environment
High school diploma	Minimum Education Level
$12,200 to $16,670 to $23,560+	Salary Range
Voluntary	Certification or Licensing
Faster than the average	Outlook

Overview

Nurse assistants (nurse aides, orderlies, or hospital attendants) work under the supervision of nurses and handle much of the personal care needs of the patients. This allows the nursing staff to perform their primary duties more effectively and efficiently. Nurse assistants help move patients, assist in patients' exercise and nutrition needs, and oversee patients' personal hygiene. Nurse assistants may also be required to take patients to other areas of the hospital for treatment, therapy, or diagnostic testing. They are required to keep charts of their work with their patients for review by other medical personnel and to comply with required reporting.

The Job

Today, there are about 1.4 million nurse assistants in the United States, and about half of them are employed in nursing homes. Nurse assistants generally help nurses care for patients in hospital or nursing home settings. Their duties include tending to the daily care of the patients, including bathing, helping them with their meals, and checking their body temperature and blood pressure. In addition, they often help persons who need assistance with their personal hygiene needs and answer their call lights when they need immediate assistance.

The work can be strenuous, requiring the lifting and moving of patients. Nurse assistants must work with partners or in groups when performing the more strenuous tasks to ensure their safety as well as the patient's. Some requirements of the job can be as routine as changing sheets and helping a patient or resident with phone calls, while other requirements can be as difficult and unattractive as assisting a resident with elimination and cleaning up a resident or patient who has vomited.

Nurse assistants may be called upon to perform the more menial and unappealing tasks of health and personal care, but they also have the opportunity to develop meaningful relationships with residents. In a nursing home, nursing assistants work closely with patients, often gaining their trust and admiration.

Requirements

High School

Communication skills are valuable for a nurse assistant. Science courses, such as biology and anatomy, will help prepare you for future training. Because a high school diploma is not required for nurse assistants, many high school students are hired by nursing homes and hospitals for part-time work. Job opportunities may also exist in a hospital or nursing home kitchen, introducing you to diet and nutrition. These jobs will also give you an opportunity to become familiar with the hospital and nursing home environments. Also, volunteer work can familiarize you with the work environment of nurses and nurse assistants, as well as introduce you to medical terminology.

Postsecondary Training

Nurse assistants are not required to have a college degree, but they may have to complete a short training course at a community college or vocational school. These training courses, usually taught by a registered nurse, teach basic nursing skills and prepare students for the state certification exam. Nurse assistants typically begin the training courses after getting their first job as an assistant, and the course work is often incorporated into their on-the-job training.

Many people work as nurse assistants as they pursue other medical professions such as a premedical or nursing program.

Certification or Licensing

Some states require nurse assistants to be certified no matter where they work. The Omnibus Budget Reconciliation Act (OBRA) passed by Congress in 1987 requires nursing homes to hire only certified nurse assistants. OBRA also requires continuing education and periodic evaluations for nurse assistants.

Other Requirements

You must care about the patients in your care and you must show a genuine understanding and compassion for the ill, disabled, and the elderly. Because of the rigorous physical demands placed on you, you should be in good health and have good work habits. Along with good physical health, you should have good mental health and a cheerful disposition. The job can be emotionally demanding, requiring patience and stability. You should be able to work as a part of a team and also be able to take orders and follow through on your responsibilities.

Exploring

Because a high school diploma is not required of nursing aides, many high school students are hired by nursing homes and hospitals for part-time work. Job opportunities may also exist in a hospital or nursing home kitchen, introducing you to diet and nutrition. Also, volunteer work can familiarize you with the work nurses and nurse assistants perform, as well as introduce you to some medical terminology.

Employers

Over one-half of nurse assistants are employed in nursing homes. Others are employed in hospitals, halfway houses, retirement centers, homes for persons with disabilities, and private homes.

Starting Out

Because of the high demand for nurse assistants, you can apply directly to the health facilities in your area, contact your local employment office, or check your local newspaper's help wanted ads.

Advancement

For the most part, there is not much opportunity for advancement with this job. To advance in a health care facility requires additional training. After becoming familiar with the medical and nursing home environments and gaining some knowledge of medical terminology, some nurse assistants enroll in nursing programs or pursue other medically related careers.

Many facilities are recognizing the need to retain good health care workers and are putting some training and advancement programs in place for their employees.

Earnings

Salaries for most health care professionals vary by region, population, and size and kind of institution. The pay for nurse assistants in a hospital is usually more than in a nursing home.

According to the *Occupational Outlook Handbook,* in 1998, nurse assistants earned average hourly earnings of $7.99, or about $16,620 annually. The lowest 10 percent earned $5.87 an hour or less, while the highest 10 percent earned more than $11.33 per hour. Nurse assistants who worked in hospitals averaged $8.10 per hour, or about $16,850 per year.

Benefits are usually based on the hours worked, length of employment, and the policies of the facility. Some offer paid vacation and holidays, medical or hospital insurance, and retirement plans. Some also provide free meals to their workers.

Work Environment

The work environment in a health care or long-term care facility can be hectic at times and very stressful. Some patients may be uncooperative and may actually be combative. Often there are numerous demands that must be met at the same time. You are required to be on your feet most of the time and you often have to help lift or move patients. Most facilities are clean and well lighted, but you do have the possibility of exposure to contagious diseases although using proper safety procedures minimizes your risk.

Nurse assistants generally work a 40-hour workweek, with some overtime. The hours and weekly schedule may be irregular, depending on the needs of the institution. Nurse assistants are needed around the clock, so work schedules may include night shift or swing-shift work.

Outlook

There will continue to be many job opportunities for nurse assistants. Because of the physical and emotional demands of the job, and because of the lack of advancement opportunities without further training, there is a high employee turnover rate. Opportunities for nurse assistants will be particularly good in nursing and personal care facilities. Additional opportunities may be available as different types of care facilities are developed and as facilities try to curb operating costs.

In addition, more nurse assistants will be required as government and private agencies develop more programs to assist people with disabilities, dependent people, and the increasing aging population.

For More Information

The following organization provides information on nurse assistant careers and training.

Career Nurse Assistants' Program, Inc.
3577 Easton Road
Norton, OH 44203-5661
Tel: 330-825-9342
Email: Info-CNA@cna-network.org
Web: http://www.cna-network.org

Nurse Managers

Biology Chemistry	School Subjects
Helping/teaching Technical/scientific	Personal Interests
Primarily indoors Primarily one location	Work Environment
Some postsecondary training	Minimum Education Level
$30,000 to $50,000 to $75,000	Salary Range
Required by all states	Certification or Licensing
Faster than the average	Outlook

Overview

Nurse managers are experienced health care professionals who manage the operations of services and personnel in medical offices, hospitals, nursing homes, community health programs, institutions, and other places where health care is provided. Their responsibilities vary depending on their position and place of employment. They may be in charge of hiring and firing their staff, as well as evaluating their performance. They are usually responsible for maintaining patient and departmental records including government and insurance documents. They may be responsible for developing and maintaining budgets. Nurse managers are often in charge of establishing, implementing, and enforcing departmental policies.

Some nurse managers provide nursing care to patients along with managing the floor or unit. They are referred to as "working managers."

The Job

Nurse managers are leaders in the health field. They are the professionals responsible for managing the staff that cares for patients. They are also in charge of the operation of their department or unit, and perform administrative duties related to patient care.

Debbie Robertson-Huffman, RN, BSN, has 22 years of operating room experience and is currently director of surgical services for a 100-bed hospital in California. She is in charge of five departments within the surgical unit: central processing, operating room staff, ambulatory surgery, recovery room, and special procedures, such as endoscopies.

Being in charge means she is responsible for the hiring, firing, and scheduling of all of her employees, scheduling the operating and special procedures rooms, and ultimately for the smooth operation of the entire surgical unit.

Although it is demanding, Robertson-Huffman enjoys her job. She loves working with her staff. "I have the greatest people working for me," she brags. "The dependable staff I have in all my departments makes it an easy job for me. Our group is like one big, happy family—with its dysfunctional moments," she laughs.

"Nurse managers need to be people persons," notes Robertson-Huffman. "They must believe in team work and that every member of the team is essential and that no one is more, or less, important than someone else."

Although working with people is a plus, the paperwork involved is a minus. "It is so cumbersome," says Robertson-Huffman. "Someone is always needing a report or statistics. We are losing sight of the people with all of the report requirements."

Nurse managers are responsible for many aspects of the smooth operation of their unit. "I liked the ability to get things accomplished," says Sharon Stout, RN, and a nurse manager of a small pediatrics unit for four years. "I saw what needed to be done and knew who to call and what to do to get it done. I liked that."

Some nurse managers are working nurse managers, meaning that they also care directly for patients along with managing the department. Robertson-Huffman will often help out in the operating room, or as she calls it, "the heart of the OR" when she is needed. Stout was also a working nurse manager. She says the size of the facility usually determines if the nurse manager also cares for patients. "I liked being a working nurse manager," she says, "because it put me in contact with the patients and their families."

Nurse managers work long hours and are usually on call. Robertson-Huffman works 8- to 10-hour shifts, five days a week, and is always on call for situations that might arise. "Nurse managers need to have stamina," she notes.

In addition, downsizing at some health care facilities and mergers of institutions may mean additional responsibilities for nurse managers.

Requirements

Postsecondary Training

Nurse managers are required to be registered nurses. (See *Registered Nurses.*) Bachelor's or advanced degrees may be required for some nurse manager positions. Nurse managers need to have considerable clinical nursing experience and previous management experience.

Some nurses combine their nursing degree with a business degree, or take business studies or health care management courses to advance to higher management positions such as directors, health care executives, or administrators.

Other Requirements

Nurse managers must be good people managers and have the ability to work with all levels of employees and management, as well as patients and their families. They should have excellent organizational and leadership skills, and be able to make intelligent decisions in a fast-paced environment. They must also be assertive and demand that procedures are done correctly and quickly. They often need to set policies and see that they are followed and documented. New medical technologies and patient treatments are constantly being developed and implemented so nurse managers must stay abreast of new information in the medical field. They also need to stay up-to-date on new insurance and government regulations and reporting requirements.

Exploring

You can explore your interest in the nursing field in a number of ways. You can read books on careers in nursing and talk with high school guidance counselors, school nurses, and local public health nurses. Visit hospitals to observe the work and to talk with hospital personnel.

Some hospitals now have extensive volunteer service programs in which students can work after school, on weekends, or during vacations. You can find other volunteer work experiences with the Red Cross or community health services. Camp counseling jobs sometimes offer related experiences. Some schools offer participation in Future Nurses programs.

Employers

Nurses are employed by hospitals, managed-care facilities, long-term-care facilities, clinics, industry, private homes, schools, camps, and government agencies.

Starting Out

The only way to become a registered nurse is through completion of one of the three kinds of educational programs, plus passing the licensing examination. Registered nurses may apply for employment directly to hospitals, nursing homes, companies, and government agencies that hire nurses. Jobs can also be obtained through school placement offices, by signing up with employment agencies specializing in placement of nursing personnel, or through the state employment office. Other sources of jobs include nurses' associations, professional journals, and newspaper want ads.

Advancement

Administrative and supervisory positions in the nursing field go to nurses who have earned at least the bachelor of science degree in nursing. Nurses with many years of experience who are graduates of the diploma program may achieve supervisory positions, but requirements for such promotions have become more difficult in recent years and in many cases require at least the bachelor of science in nursing degree.

Earnings

Educational background, experience, responsibilities, and geographic location determine earnings as a nurse manager.

According to the U.S. Department of Labor's *Occupational Outlook Handbook*, registered nurses earned an average of $40,690 annually in 1998. The low 10 percent earned less than $29,480, while the middle 50 percent earned between $34,430 and $49,070. The top 10 percent made over $69,300 a year. However, nurse managers can expect to make more. Some nurse managers advance into administrative or director positions where their salary is even higher.

Employers usually provide health and life insurance, and some offer educational reimbursements.

Work Environment

Nurse managers can work in any number of health care facilities including doctor's offices, medical clinics, hospitals, institutions, and nursing homes, as well as other medical facilities. Most health care environments are clean and well lighted. Inner city facilities may be in less than desirable locations and safety may be an issue.

All health-related careers have some health and disease risks; however, adherence to health and safety guidelines greatly minimizes the chance of contracting infectious diseases such as hepatitis and AIDS. Medical knowledge and good safety measures are also needed to limit exposure to toxic chemicals, radiation, and other hazards.

Outlook

Nursing specialties will be in great demand in the future. The U.S. Bureau of Labor Statistics lists nursing as one of 10 occupations with the largest growth rate. From 1998 to 2008, jobs for registered nurses are expected to increase by 21.6 percent. In addition, the unemployment rate for all nursing professions according to the American Association of Critical Care Nurses is less than 2 percent. These statistics support the need for nurse managers today and in the future.

For More Information

American Association of Colleges of Nursing
One Dupont Circle, NW, Suite 530
Washington, DC 20036
Tel: 202-463-6930
Web: http://www.aacn.nche.edu

American Organization of Nurse Executives
One North Franklin
Chicago, IL 60606
Tel: 312-422-2800
Web: http://www.aone.org

Nurse Practitioners

	School Subjects
Biology Chemistry	
	Personal Skills
Helping/teaching Technical/scientific	
	Work Environment
Primarily indoors Primarily multiple locations	
	Minimum Education Level
Master's degree	
	Salary Range
$34,000 to $45,000 to $60,000	
	Certification or Licensing
Voluntary	
	Outlook
Faster than the average	

Overview

Nurse practitioners are one of four classifications of advanced practice nurses (APNs). (See *Advanced Practice Nurses*.) APNs are registered nurses who have advanced training and education. This training enables them to carry out many of the responsibilities traditionally handled by physicians. Currently there are approximately 71,000 nurse practitioners in the United States. Some nurse practitioners specialize in a certain field, such as pediatrics, oncology, critical care, or primary care. The most common specialty is a family nurse practitioner who usually serves community-based health clinics.

History

Nurse practitioners first appeared on the scene following World War II, partially in response to the acute shortage of physicians. In addition, there was an influx of former corpsmen who hoped to utilize their military training and experience to fill the void of medical practitioners.

Even prior to the establishment of the first training program for nurse practitioners at Duke University in 1965, nurses had performed simple but time-consuming tasks formerly regarded as the physician's responsibility, such as taking blood pressures or administering intravenous feedings or medications. Those involved in the first nurse practitioner training program at Duke believed that nurse practitioners could perform many of the time-consuming tasks then restricted to physicians, thus freeing up the physicians to handle more complex cases.

The nurse practitioner has also fulfilled a need to focus more on health maintenance and illness prevention. In 1986, a study carried out by the U.S. Congress Office of Technology Assessment found that "within their areas of competence, nurse practitioners provide care whose quality is equivalent to that of care provided by physicians." In preventive care and communication with patients, nurse practitioners were found to excel doctors. Nurse practitioners are assuming an increasingly important role in the health care industry.

The Job

A nurse practitioner's responsibilities depend on the work setting and area of specialization. A nurse practitioner may work in close collaboration with a physician at a hospital, health center, or private practice office. Sometimes, as in the case of rural health care providers, they may only have weekly telephone contact with a physician. Eighteen states allow nurse practitioners to function entirely independent of a physician. In all states, a nurse practitioner may write prescriptions, but a physician's signature is often required to validate the prescription.

Family nurse practitioners (FNP) are often based in community health clinics. They provide primary care to people of all ages, assessing, diagnosing, and treating common illnesses and injuries. Their interactions with patients have a strong emphasis on teaching and counseling for health maintenance. Nurse practitioners recognize the importance of the social and emotional aspects of health care in addition to the more obvious physical factors.

Nurse practitioners in other specialties perform similar tasks, although they may work with different age groups or with people in schools or institutional settings. Just as physicians do, nurse practitioners select a field of specialization. A *pediatric nurse practitioner* (PNP) provides primary health care for infants through adolescents. *Gerontological nurse practitioners* are often based in nursing homes and work with older adults. *School nurse practitioners* work in school settings and provide primary health care for students.

Occupational health nurse practitioners focus on employment-related health problems and injuries. *Psychiatric nurse practitioners* work with people who have mental or emotional problems. *Women's health care nurse practitioners* provide primary care for women from adolescence through old age and may provide services from contraception to hormone replacement therapy.

Requirements

Postsecondary Training

You must be a registered nurse (RN) before you can become a nurse practitioner. (See *Registered Nurses.*) Admission to good nurse practitioner programs is very competitive. A master's degree is usually required to become a nurse practitioner. Nurse practitioner programs last one to two years and provide advanced study in diagnostic skills, health assessment, pharmacology, clinical management, and research skills. Usually the student begins with generalist work and later focuses on a specific nurse practitioner specialty.

Certification or Licensing

National certification exams for nurse practitioners are available and strongly recommended by professional organizations. At least 36 states require NPs to be nationally certified by the American Nursing Association (ANA) or a specialty nursing association. In the mid-1990s, about 58 percent of NPs were certified by various nursing organizations.

Other Requirements

To be a good nurse practitioner you should enjoy working with people and be strongly committed to making a positive difference in people's lives. You must develop excellent communication skills and should have patience, flexibility, and the ability to remain calm in an emergency. Since you may work independently much of the time, you need to be able to take active responsibility in health care situations and have good judgment regarding these situations. Your role will be strongly focused on health maintenance and prevention so you should enjoy teaching and counseling as well.

Exploring

You can explore your interest in the nursing field in a number of ways. You can read books on careers in nursing and talk with high school guidance counselors, school nurses, and local public health nurses. Visit hospitals to observe the work and to talk with hospital personnel.

Some hospitals now have extensive volunteer service programs in which students can work after school, on weekends, or during vacations. You can find other volunteer work experiences with the Red Cross or community health services. Camp counseling jobs sometimes offer related experiences. Some schools offer participation in Future Nurses programs.

Employers

Nurses are employed by hospitals, managed-care facilities, long-term-care facilities, clinics, industry, private homes, schools, camps, and government agencies.

Starting Out

The only way to become a registered nurse is through completion of one of the three kinds of educational programs, plus passing the licensing examination. Registered nurses may apply for employment directly to hospitals, nursing homes, companies, and government agencies that hire nurses. Jobs can also be obtained through school placement offices, by signing up with employment agencies specializing in placement of nursing personnel, or through the state employment office. Other sources of jobs include nurses' associations, professional journals, and newspaper want ads.

Advancement

Administrative and supervisory positions in the nursing field go to nurses who have earned at least the bachelor of science degree in nursing. Nurses with many years of experience who are graduates of the diploma program may achieve supervisory positions, but requirements for such promotions have become more difficult in recent years and in many cases require at least the bachelor of science in nursing degree.

Earnings

Geographical location and experience are factors in salary levels. Salaries for nurse practitioners, according to the National Alliance of Nurse Practitioners, range from $45,000 to $60,000.

Full-time nurse practitioners can usually expect benefits and time off that are standard for the health care profession. Benefits for part-time workers usually vary more widely and can include sick days, vacation time, and insurance.

Work Environment

The work environment depends on the nurse practitioner's specialty. Some work in remote, rural settings in small, local health care clinics. Others work in modern hospitals or nursing homes. Some nurse practitioners may work with patients who are fearful of any type of health care provider or who may have never been to a clinic before. Some patients may resent being seen by "just a nurse" instead of the doctor. Others may work with medical staff who are uncooperative and who feel threatened by the role of the nurse practitioner. All of these situations require tact, patience, and maturity.

Nurse practitioners must often work long and inconvenient hours, especially if they are involved in rural health care.

Outlook

The job outlook for nurse practitioners is excellent, since the nurse practitioner is increasingly being recognized as a provider of the high quality yet cost-effective medical care that the nation's health care system needs. In addition, more and more people are recognizing the importance of preventive health care, which is one of the nurse practitioner's greatest strengths. There should be an especially strong demand for gerontological nurse practitioners as the percentage of the U.S. population in the over-65 age group increases.

Some health care professionals report increasing frustration with recent cutbacks in the health care industry that make it difficult to persuade insurance companies to approve some health care treatments. However, nurse practitioner organizations are working to promote legislation that will increase the degree of autonomy available to nurse practitioners and make it easier for them to receive insurance company reimbursement. This should make the profession an even more attractive advancement route for RNs.

For More Information

The following organizations provide information on nurse practitioner careers.

American Academy of Nurse Practitioners
Capitol Station, LBJ Building
PO Box 12846
Austin, TX 78711
Tel: 512-442-4262
Email: admin@aanp.org
Web: http://www.aanp.org

National Alliance of Nurse Practitioners
325 Pennsylvania Avenue, SE
Washington, DC 20003
Tel: 202-675-6350

Nursing Instructors

School Subjects
- Biology
- Chemistry

Personal Interests
- Helping/teaching
- Technical/scientific

Work Environment
- Primarily indoors
- Primarily multiple locations

Minimum Education Level
- Bachelor's degree

Salary Range
- $30,000 to $50,000 to $90,000

Certification or Licensing
- Required by all states

Outlook
- Faster than the average

Overview

Nursing instructors teach patient care to nursing students in classroom and clinical settings. They demonstrate care methods and monitor hands-on learning by their students. They instruct students in the principles and applications of biological and psychological subjects related to nursing. Some nursing instructors specialize in teaching specific areas of nursing such as surgical or oncological nursing.

Nursing instructors may be full professors, assistant professors, instructors, or lecturers depending on their education and the facilities' nursing programs.

The Job

Nursing instructors teach in colleges and universities, or nursing schools. They teach in classrooms and in clinical settings. Their duties depend on the facility, the nursing program, and the instructor's education level. Some nursing instructors specialize in specific subjects such as chemistry or anatomy, or in a type of nursing activity such as pediatric nursing.

Many health care facilities partner with area nursing programs so the students can actually practice what they are learning under the supervision of nursing staff and instructors. For example, the students may spend time in a hospital environment learning pediatrics and surgical care, and additional time in a nursing home setting learning the health care needs of the elderly and handicapped. Classroom instruction and clinical training depend on the nursing program and the degree conferred.

Mary Bell, RN, who has 12 years of nursing experience, taught classes part-time as an associate professor in Indiana. Classroom teaching and clinical practice were her responsibilities.

Bell says, "As part of the clinical instruction, students conferred with me regarding the patients. They assessed the patients and learned how to chart information and statistics. Sometimes their patient observations were very keen."

"I loved the clinical part of teaching," she says. "The students often brought a new perspective to nursing. They were always eager to learn and to share what they learned.

"Nursing technology and care is always changing and the instructor shouldn't mind being challenged," states Bell. She goes on to say that the instructor must be able to create dialogue so there is an exchange of information and ideas. "It is a process between student and teacher," she observes.

Nursing instructors must spend a lot of preparation time outside the classroom and clinical setting according to Bell. For example, the instructor must work with head nurses or charge nurses to determine the students' patient assignments. They must review patients' charts and be well informed about their current conditions prior to the student nurses appearing for their clinical instruction. Plus, there are the usual teaching responsibilities such as course planning, paper grading, and test preparation. Involvement often extends beyond the classroom.

"Professors at universities and colleges are expected to be involved with the community," says Bell. They may be required to speak to community groups or consult with businesses, and are encouraged to be active in professional associations and on academic committees.

"In addition, many larger institutions expect professors to do research and be published in nursing or medical journals," Bell notes.

Teaching load and research requirements vary by institution and program. Full professors usually spend more of their time conducting research and publishing than assistant professors, instructors, and lecturers.

Often nursing instructors actively work in the nursing field along with teaching. "They will do this to maintain current hands-on experience and to advance their careers," Bell acknowledges. "It is a huge commitment."

"But," she adds, "it's great being able to see the light bulb turn on in the students' heads."

Requirements

Postsecondary Training

Nursing instructors may be required to be registered nurses. (See *Registered Nurses*.) Nursing instructors should have considerable clinical nursing experience before considering teaching.

Almost all universities and colleges require that their full-time professors have doctoral degrees, but many hire master's degree holders for part-time and temporary teaching positions. Two-year colleges may hire full-time teachers who have master's degrees. Smaller institutions or nursing schools may hire part-time nursing instructors who have a bachelor's degree.

Other Requirements

Nursing instructors must enjoy teaching and nursing. They should have excellent organizational and leadership skills, and be able to communicate well with professional staff and students of all ages. They should be able to demonstrate skilled nursing techniques. They must have good supervision skills since they are responsible for all the care their students administer to patients. In addition, they should be able to teach their students the humane side of nursing that is so important in patient and nurse relationships. New medical technologies, patient treatments, and medications are constantly being developed, so nursing instructors must stay abreast of new information in the medical field. They need to be up-to-date on the use of new medical equipment that is used for patient care.

Exploring

You can explore your interest in the nursing field in a number of ways. You can read books on careers in nursing and talk with high school guidance counselors, school nurses, and local public health nurses. Visit hospitals to observe the work and to talk with hospital personnel.

Some hospitals now have extensive volunteer service programs in which students can work after school, on weekends, or during vacations. You can find other volunteer work experiences with the Red Cross or community health services. Camp counseling jobs sometimes offer related experiences. Some schools offer participation in Future Nurses programs.

Employers

Nurses are employed by hospitals, managed-care facilities, long-term-care facilities, clinics, industry, private homes, schools, camps, and government agencies.

Starting Out

The only way to become a registered nurse is through completion of one of the three kinds of educational programs, plus passing the licensing examination. Registered nurses may apply for employment directly to hospitals, nursing homes, companies, and government agencies that hire nurses. Jobs can also be obtained through school placement offices, by signing up with employment agencies specializing in placement of nursing personnel, or through the state employment office. Other sources of jobs include nurses' associations, professional journals, and newspaper want ads.

Advancement

Administrative and supervisory positions in the nursing field go to nurses who have earned at least the bachelor of science degree in nursing. Nurses with many years of experience who are graduates of the diploma program may achieve supervisory positions, but requirements for such promotions have become more difficult in recent years and in many cases require at least the bachelor of science in nursing degree.

Earnings

Educational background, experience, responsibilities, geographic location, and the hiring institution determine the earnings as a nursing instructor.

According to a survey conducted in 1998 by the American Association of Colleges of Nursing, the salaries for nursing instructors with doctoral degrees ranged from $26,000 in a public institution to $138,175 for a professor in a private secular school. Salaries for instructors who did not have doctorates ranged from $16,102 to $89,771. The survey also noted that salaries vary by type of institution and geographic location.

Employers usually provide health and life insurance and other benefits to their full-time employees.

Work Environment

Nursing instructors work in colleges, universities, or nursing schools. Their clinical instruction can take place in any number of health care facilities including doctors' offices, medical clinics, hospitals, institutions, and nursing homes. Most health care environments are clean and well lighted. Inner city facilities may be in less than desirable locations and safety may be an issue.

All health-related careers have some health and disease risks; however, adherence to health and safety guidelines greatly minimizes the chance of contracting infectious diseases such as hepatitis and AIDS. Medical knowledge and good safety measures are also needed to limit exposure to toxic chemicals, radiation, and other hazards.

Outlook

Nursing specialties will be in great demand in the future thus creating a demand for nursing instructors. The U.S. Bureau of Labor Statistics lists nursing as one of 10 occupations with the largest growth rate. From 1998 to 2008, jobs for registered nurses are expected to increase by 21.6 percent. The bureau also reports that health services is one of the largest industries in the country, and that 12 out of 30 occupations projected to grow the fastest are concentrated in health services.

These facts support the need for nurse instructors today and in the future.

For More Information

American Association of Colleges of Nursing
One Dupont Circle, NW, Suite 530
Washington, DC 20024
Tel: 202-463-6930
Web: http://www.aacn.nche.edu

American Nurses Association
600 Maryland Avenue, SW
Suite 100 West
Washington, DC 60606
Tel: 800-274-4262
Web: http://www.ana.org/

Occupational Health Nurses

School Subjects
- Biology
- Chemistry

Personal Interests
- Helping/teaching
- Technical/scientific

Work Environment
- Can be one location
- Can be multiple locations with some travel

Minimum Education Level
- Some postsecondary training

Salary Range
- $30,000 to $50,000 to $80,000

Certification or Licensing
- Required by all states

Outlook
- Faster than the average

Overview

Occupational health nurses are registered nurses who care for people in the workplace. Although they treat illnesses, injuries, and health problems, they are also involved with safety and health issues, and prevention programs. An occupational health nurse may be an employee of a business, institution, or corporation or may be self-employed on a contract or freelance basis. Some nurses may be a part of a team or company that provides occupational health services on a retainer or contract basis.

The Job

Occupational health nurses are responsible for providing health care services to the working population. These services may include emergency care in the case of an accident or critical illness, caring for ongoing work-related injuries such as back strain, or monitoring a worker's persistent high blood pressure or diabetes. The occupational health nurse may also be responsible for assessing safety aspects of the workplace. Treating injuries may include analyzing how and why the injury occurred as well as initiating preventive measures in the plant or workplace.

On-site occupational health nurses may be required to treat illnesses and injuries and respond quickly to emergency situations or industrial accidents. They may also consult with an employee regarding medical insurance coverage, an ongoing health problem such as high blood pressure, and they may serve as a one-on-one resource for general health and wellness information.

According to Cecelia Vaughn, RN, and a Certified Occupational Health Nurse Specialist (COHN-S) who works on a contract basis with a wide variety of clients, "When I go into a facility I have to look at all aspects of the work environment. Is the air clean? Is the worker exposed to harmful pollutants? Is the workplace lighting and ventilation satisfactory? Are workers tested periodically for chemical exposure, if necessary? Are safety programs presented on a regular basis?"

"And," she adds, "I need to be able to relate personally to the workers. Are they stressed? Is the woman who has bruises a victim of abuse at home? Is a worker on drugs? Is there potential for violence at the workplace?"

Along with all the assessments and intervention, the occupational health nurse is often responsible for making sure the company is following and documenting government-required workplace and health regulations. The occupational health nurse may also be involved with company-sponsored health and safety workshops, and may administer flu shots, be responsible for drug testing, and arrange for in-house mammograms and other wellness programs.

Like every nursing job, documentation and administration are important aspects of the duties. The occupational health nurse may be responsible for reporting and documenting worker's compensation claims and for making sure the company meets Occupational Safety and Health Act (OSHA) requirements, or other government workplace regulations.

The occupational health nurse may get involved with workers who have special needs to ensure that the workers have safe, accommodating workstations.

Teaching and demonstrating are a big part of an occupational nurse's responsibilities. An occupational health nurse or environmental nurse may also go into a workplace and teach the proper way to lift heavy equipment to prevent back injury, or train workers in CPR or emergency procedures.

"My job is so much fun," Vaughn says enthusiastically. "Every day is a new challenge. I never know what the day will bring and my plans can change so quickly. If a company calls with an emergency situation, I might have to drop everything and go there."

Requirements

Postsecondary Training

Nurse practitioners who specialize in a specific nursing field must first become registered nurses. (See *Registered Nurses*.)

It is preferred that nurses entering the occupational nursing field have a bachelor's degree in nursing and nursing experience, especially in community health, ambulatory care, critical care, or emergency nursing.

Other Requirements

Because the duties of an occupational health nurse are so varied and unpredictable, the ability to "think outside of the box" is critical according to Vaughn. "You must be able to look around a company and see the safety issues and the human issues, as well as the health issues. You must think about social responsibility. Is the work environment safe? Are harmful chemicals present? What emotional issues might employees be dealing with?" She adds, "This is a totally different kind of nursing than hospital bedside nursing."

Occupational health nurses should be able to think independently and make decisions quickly. They should have good management skills as well as the ability to relate well to all people in all positions.

Exploring

You can explore your interest in the nursing field in a number of ways. You can read books on careers in nursing and talk with high school guidance counselors, school nurses, and local public health nurses. Visit hospitals to observe the work and to talk with hospital personnel.

Some hospitals now have extensive volunteer service programs in which students can work after school, on weekends, or during vacations. You can find other volunteer work experiences with the Red Cross or community health services. Camp counseling jobs sometimes offer related experiences. Some schools offer participation in Future Nurses programs.

Employers

Nurses are employed by hospitals, managed-care facilities, long-term-care facilities, clinics, industry, private homes, schools, camps, and government agencies.

Starting Out

The only way to become a registered nurse is through completion of one of the three kinds of educational programs, plus passing the licensing examination. Registered nurses may apply for employment directly to hospitals, nursing homes, companies, and government agencies that hire nurses. Jobs can also be obtained through school placement offices, by signing up with employment agencies specializing in placement of nursing personnel, or through the state employment office. Other sources of jobs include nurses' associations, professional journals, and newspaper want ads.

Advancement

Administrative and supervisory positions in the nursing field go to nurses who have earned at least the bachelor of science degree in nursing. Nurses with many years of experience who are graduates of the diploma program may achieve supervisory positions, but requirements for such promotions have become more difficult in recent years and in many cases require at least the bachelor of science in nursing degree.

Earnings

According to the U.S. Department of Labor's *Occupational Outlook Handbook,* registered nurses earned an average of $40,690 annually in 1998. The low 10 percent earned less than $29,480, while the middle 50 percent earned between $34,430 and $49,070. The top 10 percent made over $69,300 a year. However, occupational health nurses can generally expect to earn more.

Salary is determined by many factors, including nursing specialty, education, and place of employment, geographical location, and work experience. Flexible schedules and part-time employment opportunities are available for most nurses. Employers usually provide health and life insurance, and some offer educational reimbursements and year-end bonuses to their full-time staff.

Work Environment

Occupational health nurses work in a variety of environments from clean, healthy, well-lighted buildings, to dusty, dirty, fume-filled manufacturing and mining facilities. Some nurses may have to spend time in hot plants analyzing safety and environmental aspects of the workplace.

All nursing careers have some health and disease risks; however, adherence to health and safety guidelines greatly minimizes the chance of contracting infectious diseases such as hepatitis and AIDS. Medical knowledge and good safety measures are also needed to limit the nurse's exposure to toxic chemicals, radiation, and other hazards

Outlook

Nursing specialties will be in great demand in the future. The U.S. Bureau of Labor Statistics lists nursing as one of 10 occupations with the largest growth rate. From 1998 to 2008, jobs for registered nurses are expected to increase by 21.6 percent.

More and more companies are realizing the value of healthy and happy employees who work in safe, environmentally conscious workplaces. While these views support the need for companies to hire occupational health nurses, the reality is that some companies see eliminating the in-house occupational health nurse as a way to save money. This downsizing then creates a need for outsourcing, which may increase the employment opportunities for independent occupational nurses or those employed with contract service companies.

The fact that we are becoming an older working America means new demands and new problems in the work force. "We are now dealing with workers in their 60s and 70s," says Vaughn. "This fact alone creates additional justification for the services of the occupational health nurse."

For More Information

American Association of Colleges of Nursing
One Dupont Circle, NW, Suite 530
Washington, DC 20036
Tel: 202-463-6930
Fax: 202-785-8320
Web: http://www.aacn.ache.edu

American Association of Occupational Health Nurses, Inc.
2920 Brandywine Road, Suite 100
Atlanta, GA 30341
Tel: 770-455-7757
Web: http://www.aaohn.org

Oncological Nurses

Biology Chemistry	School Subjects
Helping/teaching Technical/scientific	Personal Interests
Primarily indoors Primarily one location	Work Environment
Some postsecondary training	Minimum Education Level
$30,000 to $50,000 to $75,000	Salary Range
Required by all states	Certification or Licensing
Faster than the average	Outlook

Overview

Oncological nurses specialize in the treatment and care of cancer patients. While many oncological nurses care directly for cancer patients, some may be involved in patient or community education, cancer prevention, or cancer research. They may work in specific areas of cancer nursing, such as pediatrics, cancer rehabilitation, chemotherapy, biotherapy, hospice, pain management. and others. Oncological nurses practice in many professional settings, including AIDS, oncology, and medical surgical units, at hospitals and cancer centers or treatment facilities. Some may be employed by private practice physicians, hospice programs, or by health education centers or research facilities. Some may work as public health nurses.

The Job

Carolyn Panhorst, RN, BSN, worked as an oncological nurse in a small hospital in a small farming community in Indiana. "Our hospital was a satellite facility for a larger hospital in a metro area," states Panhorst. "Our doctors' offices were in the hospital and I administered chemotherapy both to patients who were admitted to the hospital and to outpatients."

Because cancer treatment and care differ considerably depending on the facilities and the type of cancer the patient has, oncological nurses' job responsibilities vary greatly. It is important for them to keep up on current research, treatments, and other advances with the disease. Nurses who must administer drugs and other types of treatment must be aware of the changes in dosages, equipment, and side effects.

Panhorst relates, "Although technical expertise is definitely required when caring for cancer patients, the nurse needs to be emotionally and personally attached to the patient. If the nurse cannot give much of herself or himself, this is felt by the patient."

Caring for patients with cancer can be an emotional nursing experience. Nurses must be aware of the psychological aspects of this type of nursing. They also need to know the effects that this disease can have on the patients, families, and friends.

"Don't get into this area and think you are going to save anybody," a nurse once told Panhorst. "I thought this was cold," she says, "but I understand now.

"You have to want to be there for your patients even though you may not be able to help them," says Panhorst. "You try to give them what science and technology knows, and then provide them with the best nursing care possible. But, you have to know that you are not God and leave your mind open to the full reality of what the possible outcome may be." She adds, "You must be satisfied that you did the best you could.

"Taking care of cancer patients is a different kind of nursing," observes Panhorst. "In normal relationships people tend to be protective, but when patients are frightened by their illness, their pretense is gone. They have the ability to communicate more openly. They trust you with their innermost feelings and that's a huge responsibility and also a privilege."

There are so many treatment choices available for cancer patients today that the nurse needs to be an educator as well as a caregiver. The nurse must help the patients receive the best possible care and also respect their wishes. "You need to be a patient advocate," says Panhorst. "You have to know the difference between giving them information and advising.

"This is an area of nursing where you can easily fall in love with your patient and their family," says Panhorst. "You can have a wonderful, meaningful relationship with the patient."

Requirements

Postsecondary Training

Oncological nurses must be registered nurses. (See *Registered Nurses*.) Entry-level requirements to become an oncological nurse depend on individual hiring qualifications of the institution or practice, and the availability of nurses in that specialty and geographical region.

Certification or Licensing

Some institutions may require certification as an oncology nurse. There are three types of certification available through the Oncology Nursing Society. The OCN (Oncology Certified Nurse) examination is aimed at testing basic knowledge within the specialty of oncology nursing. The CPON (Certified Pediatric Oncology Nurse) examination tests knowledge in pediatric oncology. The AOCN (Advanced Oncology Certified Nurse) certification is advanced certification and tests knowledge in advanced cancer nursing practices. Each specialty requires recertification.

Other Requirements

Oncological nurses should like working in a fast-paced environment that requires life-long learning. New medical technology and treatment methods are constantly being developed and implemented. Oncological nurses should be technically inclined and be able to learn how to operate new medical equipment without feeling intimidated.

Because of the seriousness of their loved one's illness, family members and friends may be difficult to deal with and the nurse must display patience, understanding, compassion, and composure during these emotional times. The nurse must be able to communicate and explain medical terminology and procedures to the patient and family so they can make informed decisions and understand what is being done and why.

Exploring

You can explore your interest in the nursing field in a number of ways. You can read books on careers in nursing and talk with high school guidance counselors, school nurses, and local public health nurses. Visit hospitals to observe the work and to talk with hospital personnel.

Some hospitals now have extensive volunteer service programs in which students can work after school, on weekends, or during vacations. You can find other volunteer work experiences with the Red Cross or community health services. Camp counseling jobs sometimes offer related experiences. Some schools offer participation in Future Nurses programs.

Employers

Nurses are employed by hospitals, managed-care facilities, long-term-care facilities, clinics, industry, private homes, schools, camps, and government agencies.

Starting Out

The only way to become a registered nurse is through completion of one of the three kinds of educational programs, plus passing the licensing examination. Registered nurses may apply for employment directly to hospitals, nursing homes, companies, and government agencies that hire nurses. Jobs can also be obtained through school placement offices, by signing up with employment agencies specializing in placement of nursing personnel, or through the state employment office. Other sources of jobs include nurses' associations, professional journals, and newspaper want ads.

Advancement

Administrative and supervisory positions in the nursing field go to nurses who have earned at least the bachelor of science degree in nursing. Nurses with many years of experience who are graduates of the diploma program may achieve supervisory positions, but requirements for such promotions have become more difficult in recent years and in many cases require at least the bachelor of science in nursing degree.

Earnings

According to the U.S. Department of Labor's *Occupational Outlook Handbook,* registered nurses earned an average of $40,690 annually in 1998. The low 10 percent earned less than $29,480, while the middle 50 percent earned between $34,430 and $49,070. The top 10 percent made over $69,300 a year. However, oncological nurses in certain areas may earn more.

Salary is determined by many factors, including nursing specialty, education, and place of employment, shift worked, geographical location, and work experience. Flexible schedules and part-time employment opportunities are available for most nurses. Employers usually provide health and life insurance, and some offer educational reimbursements and year-end bonuses to their full-time staff.

Work Environment

Oncological nurses work in various hospital and clinic settings. Most hospital environments are clean and well lighted. However, inner city hospitals may be in a less than desirable location and safety may be an issue.

Some community health nurses may work in clean, well-lighted buildings in upscale communities, while others may find themselves working in remote, underdeveloped areas that have poor living conditions. Personal safety may be an issue at times.

Generally, oncological nurses who wish to advance in their careers will find themselves working in larger hospitals or medical centers in major cities.

All nursing careers have some health and disease risks; however, adherence to health and safety guidelines greatly minimizes the chance of contracting infectious diseases such as hepatitis and AIDS. Medical knowledge and good safety measures are also needed to limit the nurse's exposure to toxic chemicals, radiation, and other hazards.

Long hours and intense nursing demands can create "burn-out" for some nurses, meaning that they often become dissatisfied with their jobs. Fortunately, there are many areas in which nurses can use their skills, so sometimes trying a different type of nursing may be the answer.

Outlook

Nursing specialties will be in great demand in the future. The U.S. Bureau of Labor Statistics lists nursing as one of 10 occupations with the largest growth rate. From 1998 to 2008, jobs for registered nurses are expected to increase by 21.6 percent. In addition, the unemployment rate for all nursing professions according to the American Association of Critical Care Nurses is less than 2 percent.

The outlook for oncological nurses is excellent. The U.S. Bureau of the Census estimates that the number of individuals aged 65 or older will double by 2050. As our population grows older, the need for oncological nursing will increase. In addition, managed care organizations will continue to need nurses to provide health promotion and disease prevention programs to their subscribers.

Job opportunities vary across the country and may be available in all geographic areas. Home health care will be a growing nursing area. (See *Home Health Care* and *Hospice Nurses*.) More services will be delivered in a home setting and patients will receive transfusions, therapy treatments, and medications through home health visits.

For More Information

American Association of Colleges of Nursing
One Dupont Circle, NW, Suite 530
Washington, DC 20036
Tel: 202-463-6930
Web: http://www.aacn.nche.edu

Oncology Nursing Society
501 Holiday Drive
Pittsburgh, PA 15220-2749
Tel: 412-921-7373
Web: http://www.ons.org

Psychiatric Nurses

Biology Chemistry	School Subjects
Helping/teaching Technical/scientific	Personal Interests
Primarily indoors Primarily one location	Work Environment
Some postsecondary training	Minimum Education Level
$29,000 to $49,000 to $69,000	Salary Range
Required by all states	Certification or Licensing
Faster than the average	Outlook

Overview

Psychiatric nurses focus on mental health. This includes the prevention of mental illness and the maintenance of good mental health, as well as the diagnosis and treatment of mental disorders. They care for pediatric, teen, adult, and elderly patients who may have a broad spectrum of mentally and emotionally related medical needs. In addition to providing individualized nursing care, psychiatric nurses serve as consultants, conduct research, and work in management and administrative positions in institutions and corporations.

The American Psychiatric Nurses Association (APNA) states that there are close to 7,000 clinical nurse specialists (See *Clinical Nurse Specialists*) who are certified in adult and/or child and adolescent psychiatric mental health nursing.

The Job

According to the APNA, psychiatric nursing occurs at two levels—basic and advanced. Basic psychiatric nurses are registered nurses who work primarily with patients needing mental health or psychiatric care.

Advanced practice nurses also provide patient care in the psychiatric and mental health setting. Advanced practice nurses are also registered nurses but they have earned certification as *certified nurse specialists* (CNS) or have taken graduate courses to become *clinical specialists/nurse practitioners* (CNS/NP), or *psychiatric nurse practitioners* (PNP). Some of these specialists may work in supervisory or administrative positions and may, depending on their state's laws, be able to provide psychotherapy services and prescribe medications.

Psychiatric nurses perform a wide range of direct-care nursing duties for the mentally ill, emotionally disturbed, and developmentally handicapped. They may work with individuals, groups, families, and communities. They care for all people, including children, teens, adults, and the elderly. The care may be in hospitals, psychiatric and mental health facilities, in doctors' offices, in correctional institutions, in nursing homes, in shelters, and in group homes.

In addition to direct patient care, some psychiatric nurses may use their training in the community as community health nurses (See *Community Health Nurses*) or educators (See *Nursing Instructors*). They may also work for insurance or managed-care companies, or in health care institutions or government facilities in an administrative, supervisory, or research position. Other nurses may be self-employed on a consulting or contract basis.

Psychiatric nursing is a very intense nursing specialty. Patients require constant attention, mental and physical care, and monitoring.

Requirements

Postsecondary Training

Psychiatric nurses must be registered nurses. (See *Registered Nurses*.) Entry-level requirements to become a psychiatric nurse depend on the state, the institution, its size, who it serves, and the availability of nurses in that specialty and geographical region. Usually nurses must have some nursing experience before entering the psychiatric nursing field. Some institutions may require certification as a psychiatric nurse. Psychiatric nurses who wish to advance their education may take graduate level courses and become nurse specialists or nurse practitioners.

Psychiatric nurses should like working in a fast-paced environment that requires life-long learning. Research into human behavior and the brain is constantly resulting in new information regarding patient care, drug therapy, and treatments.

In many cases, psychiatric nurses are confronted with situations that may require them to act immediately, independently, and confidently, so they must have good decision-making skills. They must also be good team players and able to get along with people from all walks of life. They must work with patients and families as well as other medical, administrative, and institutional personnel.

Psychiatric nurses must be able to deal with people in a troubling time of their lives. They must be able to communicate with the families and friends of persons with mental problems who may find the illness difficult to understand. Nurses need to display patience, understanding, and composure during these emotional times.

Many facilities are requiring nurses to work 10- to 12-hour shifts, which can be very exhausting. In addition, nurses are often on call.

Exploring

You can explore your interest in the nursing field in a number of ways. You can read books on careers in nursing and talk with high school guidance counselors, school nurses, and local public health nurses. Visit hospitals to observe the work and to talk with hospital personnel.

Some hospitals now have extensive volunteer service programs in which students can work after school, on weekends, or during vacations. You can find other volunteer work experiences with the Red Cross or community health services. Camp counseling jobs sometimes offer related experiences. Some schools offer participation in Future Nurses programs.

Employers

Nurses are employed by hospitals, managed-care facilities, long-term-care facilities, clinics, industry, private homes, schools, camps, and government agencies.

Starting Out

The only way to become a registered nurse is through completion of one of the three kinds of educational programs, plus passing the licensing examination. Registered nurses may apply for employment directly to hospitals, nursing homes, companies, and government agencies that hire nurses. Jobs can also be obtained through school placement offices, by signing up with employment agencies specializing in placement of nursing personnel, or through the state employment office. Other sources of jobs include nurses' associations, professional journals, and newspaper want ads.

Advancement

Administrative and supervisory positions in the nursing field go to nurses who have earned at least the bachelor of science degree in nursing. Nurses with many years of experience who are graduates of the diploma program may achieve supervisory positions, but requirements for such promotions have become more difficult in recent years and in many cases require at least the bachelor of science in nursing degree.

Earnings

According to the U.S. Department of Labor's *Occupational Outlook Handbook,* registered nurses earned an average of $40,690 annually in 1998. The low 10 percent earned less than $29,480, while the middle 50 percent earned between $34,430 and $49,070. The top 10 percent made over $69,300 a year. However, psychiatric nurses may earn more in some areas.

Salary is determined by many factors, including nursing specialty, education, place of employment, shift worked, geographical location, and work experience. Flexible schedules and part-time employment opportunities are available for most nurses. Employers usually provide health and life insurance, and some offer educational reimbursements and year-end bonuses to their full-time staff.

Work Environment

Government institutions, corporations, businesses, nursing homes, correctional institutions, research facilities, and hospitals may employ psychiatric nurses. Most hospital and institutional environments are clean and well lighted. Inner city facilities and hospitals may be in less than desirable locations and safety may be an issue. Generally, psychiatric nurses who wish to advance in their careers will find themselves working in larger facilities in major cities.

All nursing careers have some health and disease risks; however, adherence to health and safety guidelines greatly minimizes the chance of contracting infectious diseases such as hepatitis and AIDS. Medical knowledge and good safety measures are also needed to limit the nurse's exposure to toxic chemicals, radiation, and other hazards. In addition, psychiatric nurses may be exposed to violent and unpredictable behavior, which may increase their risk of injury.

Nurses usually spend much of the day on their feet, either walking or standing. Many hospital nurses work 10- or 12-hour shifts, which can be tiring. Long hours and intense nursing demands can create burnout for some nurses, meaning that they often become dissatisfied with their jobs. Fortunately, there are many areas in which nurses can use their skills, so sometimes trying a different type of nursing may be the answer.

Outlook

U.S. Surgeon General David Satcher recently reported that mental illness is a leading cause of disability in the United States and mental disorders affect one in five Americans, including children, adolescents, adults, and the elderly. The need for psychiatric and other nursing specialties will be in great demand in the future. The U.S. Bureau of Labor Statistics lists nursing as one of 10 occupations with the largest growth rate. From 1998 to 2008, jobs for registered nurses are expected to increase by 21.6 percent. The U.S. Bureau of Labor Statistics projects that employment for registered nurses will grow faster than the average for all occupations through 2008.

The unemployment rate for all nursing professions according to the American Association of Colleges of Nursing is less than 2 percent.

For More Information

American Association of Colleges of Nursing
One Dupont Circle, NW, Suite 530
Washington, DC 20036
Tel: 202-463-6930
Fax: 202-785-8320
Web: http://www.aacn.nche.edu

American Psychiatric Nurses Association
1200 19th Street, NW, Suite 300
Washington, DC 20036-2401
Tel: 202-857-1133
Fax: 202-857-1102
Web: http://www.apna.org

Registered Nurses

School Subjects	Biology Chemistry
Personal Skills	Helping/teaching Technical/scientific
Work Environment	Primarily indoors Primarily multiple locations
Minimum Education Level	Some postsecondary training
Salary Range	$16,500 to $40,700 to $69,300+
Certification or Licensing	Required by all states
Outlook	Faster than the average

Overview

Registered nurses (RNs) help individuals, families, and groups to achieve health and prevent disease. They care for the sick and injured in hospitals and other health care facilities, physicians' offices, private homes, public health agencies, schools, camps, and industry. Some registered nurses are employed in private practice.

History

Modern ideas about hospitals and nursing as a profession did not develop until the 19th century. The life and work of Florence Nightingale (1820-1910) were a strong influence on the profession's development. Nightingale, who came from a wealthy, upper-class British family, dedicated her life to improving conditions in hospitals, beginning in an army hospital during the Crimean War. In this country, many of Nightingale's ideas were put into practice for the care of the wounded during the Civil War. The care, however, was provided by concerned individuals who nursed rather than by trained nurses. They had not received the kind of training that is required for nurses today.

The first school of nursing in the United States was founded in Boston in 1873. In 1938, New York State passed the first state law to require that practical nurses be licensed. Even though the first school for the training of practical nurses was started almost 74 years ago, and the establishment of other schools followed, the training programs lacked uniformity.

After the 1938 law was passed, a movement began to have organized training programs that would assure new standards in the field. The role and training of the nurse have undergone radical changes since the first schools were opened.

Education standards for nurses have been improving constantly since that time. Today's nurse is a highly educated, licensed health care professional. Now extended programs of training are offered throughout the country, and all states have enacted laws to assure training standards are maintained and to assure qualification for licensure. The field of nursing serves an important role as a part of the health care system.

The Job

Registered nurses work under the direct supervision of nursing departments and in collaboration with physicians. Two-thirds of all nurses work in hospitals, where they may be assigned to general, operating room, or maternity room duty. They may also care for sick children or be assigned to other hospital units, such as emergency rooms, intensive care units, or outpatient clinics. There are many different kinds of RNs.

General duty nurses work together with other members of the health care team to assess the patient's condition and to develop and implement a plan of health care. These nurses may perform such tasks as taking patients' vital signs, administering medication and injections, recording the symptoms and progress of patients, changing dressings, assisting patients with personal care, conferring with members of the medical staff, helping prepare a patient for surgery, and completing any number of duties that require skill and understanding of patients' needs.

Surgical nurses oversee the preparation of the operating room and the sterilization of instruments. They assist surgeons during operations and coordinate the flow of patient cases in operating rooms.

Maternity nurses help in the delivery room, take care of newborns in the nursery, and teach mothers how to feed and care for their babies. (See *Neonatal Nurses.*)

The activities of staff nurses are directed and coordinated by head nurses and supervisors. Heading up the entire nursing program in the hospital is the *nursing service director,* who administers the nursing program to maintain standards of patient care. (See *Nurse Managers.*) The nursing service director advises the medical staff, department heads, and the hospital administrator in matters relating to nursing services and helps prepare the department budget.

Private duty nurses may work in hospitals or in a patient's home. They are employed by the patient they are caring for or by the patient's family. Their service is designed for the individual care of one person and is carried out in cooperation with the patient's physician. (See *Home Health/Hospice Nurses.*)

✗ *Office nurses* usually work in the office of a dentist, physician, or health maintenance organization (HMO). They may be one of several nurses on the staff or the only staff nurse. If a nurse is the only staff member, this person may have to combine some clerical duties with those of nursing, such as serving as receptionist, making appointments for the doctor, helping maintain patient records, sending out monthly statements, and attending to routine correspondence. If the physician's staff is a large one that includes secretaries and clerks, the office nurse will concentrate on screening patients, assisting with examinations, supervising the examining rooms, sterilizing equipment, providing patient education, and performing other nursing duties.

Occupational health nurses, or *industrial nurses,* are an important part of many large firms. They maintain a clinic at a plant or factory and are usually occupied in rendering preventive, remedial, and educational nursing services. They work under the direction of an industrial physician, nursing director, or nursing supervisor. They may advise on accident prevention, visit employees on the job to check the conditions under which they work, and advise management about the safety of such conditions. At the plant, they render treatment in emergencies. (See *Occupational Health Nurses.*)

School nurses may work in one school or in several, visiting each for a part of the day or week. They may supervise the student clinic, treat minor cuts or injuries, or give advice on good health practices. They may examine students to detect conditions of the eyes or teeth that require attention. They also assist the school physician. (See *School Nurses.*)

Community health nurses, also called *public health nurses,* require specialized training for their duties. Their job usually requires them to spend part of the time traveling from one assignment to another. Their duties may differ greatly from one case to another. For instance, in one day they may have to instruct a class of expectant mothers, visit new parents to help them plan proper care for the baby, visit an aged patient requiring special care, and conduct a class in nutrition. They usually possess many and varied nursing skills and often are called upon to meet unexpected or unusual situations. (See *Community Health Nurses.*)

Administrators in the community health field include nursing directors, educational directors, and nursing supervisors. Some nurses go into nursing education and work with nursing students to instruct them on theories and skills they will need to enter the profession. Nursing instructors may give classroom instruction and demonstrations or supervise nursing students on hospital units. Some instructors eventually become nursing school directors, university faculty, or deans of a university degree program. Nurses also have the opportunity to direct staff development and continuing education programs for nursing personnel in hospitals. (See *Nursing Instructors.*)

Advanced practice nurses are nurses with training beyond that required to have the RN designation. There are four primary categories of nurses included in this category: certified nurse-midwives, clinical nurse specialists, nurse anesthetists, and nurse practitioners. (See *Advanced Practice Nurses.*)

Some nurses are consultants to hospitals, nursing schools, industrial organizations, and public health agencies. They advise clients on such administrative matters as staff organization, nursing techniques, curricula, and education programs. Other administrative specialists include educational directors for the state board of nursing, who are concerned with maintaining well-defined educational standards, and executive directors of professional nurses' associations, who administer programs developed by the board of directors and the members of the association.

Some nurses choose to enter the armed forces. All types of nurses, except private duty nurses, are represented in the military services. They provide skilled nursing care to active-duty and retired members of the armed forces and their families. In addition to basic nursing skills, *military nurses* are trained to provide care in various environments, including field hospitals, on-air evacuation flights, and onboard ships. Military nurses actively influence the development of health care through nursing research. Advances influenced by military nurses include the development of the artificial kidney (dialysis unit) and the concept of the intensive care unit.

Requirements

High School

High school students interested in becoming a registered nurse should take mathematics and science courses, including biology, chemistry, and physics. English and speech courses should not be neglected because the nurse must be able to communicate well with patients.

Postsecondary Training

There are three basic kinds of training programs that prospective nurses may choose to become registered nurses: associate's degree programs, diploma programs, and bachelor's degree programs. Which of the three training programs to choose depends on one's career goals. A bachelor's degree in nursing is required for most supervisory or administrative positions, for jobs in public health agencies, and for admission to graduate nursing programs. A master's degree is usually necessary to prepare for a nursing specialty or to teach. For some specialties, such as nursing research, a PhD is essential.

The bachelor's degree program is offered by colleges or universities. It requires four (in some cases, five) years to complete. The graduate of this program receives a Bachelor of Science in Nursing degree. The Associate in Arts in Nursing is awarded after completion of a two-year study program that is usually offered in a junior or community college. The student receives hospital training at cooperating hospitals in the general vicinity of the community college. The diploma program, which usually lasts three years, is conducted by hospitals and independent schools. At the conclusion of each of these programs, the student becomes a graduate nurse, but not, however, a registered nurse. To obtain the RN designation the graduate nurse must take and pass a licensing examination required in all states.

In 1998, there were over 2,200 entry-level nursing programs offered in the United States. In addition, there were 198 master's degree and 33 doctoral degree programs. Nurses can pursue postgraduate training that allows them to specialize in certain areas, such as emergency room, operating room, premature nursery, or psychiatric nursing. This training is sometimes offered through hospital on-the-job training programs.

Certification or Licensing

All states and the District of Columbia require a license to practice nursing. To obtain a license, graduates of approved nursing schools must pass a national examination. Nurses may be licensed by more than one state. In some states, continuing education is a condition for license renewal. Different titles require different education and training levels.

Exploring

High school students can explore their interest in the nursing field in a number of ways. They may read books on careers in nursing and talk with high school guidance counselors, school nurses, and local public health nurses. Visits to hospitals to observe the work and to talk with hospital personnel are also valuable.

Some hospitals now have extensive volunteer service programs in which high school students may work after school, on weekends, or during vacations in order to both render a valuable service and to explore their interests. Other volunteer work experiences may be found with the Red Cross or community health services. Camp counseling jobs sometimes offer related experiences. Some schools offer participation in Future Nurses programs.

Employers

Nurses are employed by hospitals, managed-care facilities, long-term-care facilities, clinics, industry, private homes, schools, camps, and government agencies.

Starting Out

The only way to become a registered nurse is through completion of one of the three kinds of educational programs, plus passing the licensing examination. Registered nurses may apply for employment directly to hospitals, nursing homes, companies, and government agencies that hire nurses. Jobs can also be obtained through school placement offices, by signing up with employment agencies specializing in placement of nursing personnel, or through the state employment office. Other sources of jobs include nurses' associations, professional journals, and newspaper want ads.

Advancement

Increasingly, administrative and supervisory positions in the nursing field go to nurses who have earned at least the bachelor of science degree in nursing. Nurses with many years of experience who are graduates of the diploma program may achieve supervisory positions, but requirements for such promotions have become more difficult in recent years and in many cases require at least the bachelor of science in nursing degree.

Nurses with bachelor's degrees are usually those who are hired as public health nurses. Nurses with master's degrees are often employed as clinical nurse specialists, faculty, instructors, supervisors, or administrators.

RNs can pursue further education to become advanced practice nurses, who have greater responsibilities and command higher salaries.

Earnings

According to the *Occupational Outlook Handbook,* registered nurses earned an average of $40,690 annually in 1998. Fifty percent earned between $34,430 and $49,070. The top 10 percent made more than $69,300 a year.

A Buck Survey found that staff RNs working in a nursing home setting earned an average of about $32,968 a year. Entry-level positions with the Department of Veterans Affairs started at approximately $16,500 for nurses who were graduates of the diploma program or the associate's of arts program. The average annual salary for all nurses in federal government agencies was about $26,100.

Salary is determined by several factors: setting, education, and work experience. Most full-time nurses are given flexible work schedules as well as health and life insurance; some are offered education reimbursement and year-end bonuses. A staff nurse's salary is limited only by the amount of work one is willing to take on. Many nurses take advantage of overtime work and shift differentials. About 10 percent of all nurses hold more than one job.

Work Environment

Most nurses work in facilities that are clean and well lighted and where the temperature is controlled, although some work in rundown inner city hospitals in less than ideal conditions. Usually, nurses work eight-hour shifts. Those in hospitals generally work any of three shifts: 7:00 AM to 3:00 PM; 3:00 PM to 11:00 PM; or 11:00 PM to 7:00 AM.

Nurses spend much of the day on their feet, either walking or standing. Handling patients who are ill or infirm can also be very exhausting. Nurses who come in contact with patients with infectious diseases must be especially careful about cleanliness and sterility. Although many nursing duties are routine, many responsibilities are unpredictable. Sick persons are often very demanding, or they may be depressed or irritable. Despite this, the nurse must retain her or his composure and should be cheerful to help the patient achieve emotional balance.

Community health nurses may be required to visit homes that are in poor condition or very dirty. They may also come in contact with social problems, such as family violence. The nurse is an important health care provider, and in many communities the sole provider.

Both the office nurse and the industrial nurse work regular business hours and are seldom required to work overtime. In some jobs, such as where nurses are on duty in private homes, they may frequently travel from home to home and work with various cases.

Outlook

In 1998, there were about 2.1 million nurses employed in the United States—making this field the largest of all health care occupations. Employment prospects for nurses look good. The U.S. Department of Labor projects registered nurses to be one of the top 25 occupations with fastest growth, high pay, and low unemployment. In fact, it is predicted that there will be about 451,000 additional jobs available through 2008.

Increasing numbers of nurses who have been attracted to the profession in recent years have, however, lessened the demand for nurses in some areas. Even so, there are still many employment opportunities for nurses, especially in the inner cities and in rural areas. Employment opportunities for nurses will be best in home health situations. The increased number of older people and better medical technology have spurred the demand for nurses to bring complicated treatments to the patients' homes.

Employment in nursing homes is expected to grow much faster than the average. Though more people are living well into their 80s and 90s, many need the kind of long term care available at a nursing home. Also, because of financial reasons, patients are being released from hospitals sooner and admitted into nursing homes. Many nursing homes have facilities and staff capable of caring for long term rehabilitation patients, as well as those afflicted with Alzheimer's. Many nurses will also be needed to help staff the growing number of outpatient facilities, such as HMOs, group medical practices, and ambulatory surgery centers.

Two-thirds of all nursing jobs are found in hospitals. However, because of administrative cost cutting, increased nurse's work load, and rapid growth of outpatient services, hospital nursing jobs will experience slower than average growth.

Nursing specialties will be in great demand. There are, in addition, many part-time employment possibilities—approximately 25 percent of all nurses work on a part-time basis.

For More Information

Visit the AACN Web site to access a list of member schools and to read the online pamphlet, Your Nursing Career: A Look at the Facts.

American Association of Colleges of Nursing
1 Dupont Circle, Suite 530
Washington, DC 20036
Tel: 202-463-6930
Web: http://www.aacn.nche.edu

For information about opportunities as an RN, contact:

American Nurses' Association
600 Maryland Avenue, SW, Suite 100W
Washington, DC 20024-2571
Tel: 800-274-4ANA
Web: http://www.nursingworld.org

*For information about state-approved programs and information on nursing,
contact:*

National Association for Practical Nurse Education and Service, Inc.
1400 Spring Street, Suite 310
Silver Spring, MD 20910
Tel: 301-588-2491
Email: napnes@aol.com

National League for Nursing
61 Broadway
New York, NY 10006
Tel: 800-669-1656
Email: nlnweb@nln.org
Web: http://www.nln.org/

School Nurses

School Subjects

Biology
Chemistry

Personal Interests

Helping/teaching
Technical/scientific

Work Environment

Primarily indoors
May be more than one location

Minimum Education Level

Some postsecondary training

Salary Range

$21,000 to $32,000 to $41,000

Certification or Licensing

Required by some states

Outlook

Little change or more slowly than
the average

Overview

School nurses focus on students' overall health. They may work in one school or in several, visiting each for a part of the day or week. They may also assist the school physician, if the school employs one. They work with parents, teachers, and other school and professional personnel to meet students' health needs. School nurses promote health and safety, work to prevent illnesses, treat accidents and minor injuries, maintain students' health records, and refer students who may need additional medical attention. School nurses may also be responsible for health education programs and school health plans. They are also in charge of administering medication to children and for seeing that special needs students' health requirements are met. School nurses are employed at the elementary, middle, and high school levels.

According to the Health Resources and Services Administration's latest information, there were 47,600 registered nurses employed as school nurses in public schools in the United States in 1996.

The Job

"Many people think school nursing is simply putting bandages on skinned knees, but it is much more than that," says Sue Schilb, RN, a school nurse at an elementary school in Iowa for five years. "Of course, we take care of injured and sick children, but what most people don't realize is the amount of paperwork, planning, and record keeping that is involved in the job."

Schilb adds, "We must assess every child entering kindergarten and make sure the child has had all the required immunizations. In addition, we must maintain records on all the students, including state-mandated immunizations. We take the height and weight of each student every year, check their vision, and work with an audiologist to conduct hearing tests."

In addition to all the record keeping tasks, school nurses are frequently a resource for parents or staff members. "We often interact with parents when their children are ill or if they have questions about their child's health," says Schilb. "If special needs children attend our school, we must develop a care plan for them to make sure their needs are met."

School nurses are also health educators. Teachers may ask the school nurse to speak to their individual classes when they are covering subjects that deal with health or safety. School nurses may also be required to make presentations such as disease prevention, health education, and environmental health and safety to the student body, staff, and parent organizations.

School nurses may be employed full- or part-time depending on the school's needs, their funding, their size, and their state's or district's requirements. Some school nurses may also be employed in private or parochial schools. Some school systems may have a registered school nurse who works in a management capacity and oversees health aides employed in the schools.

Requirements

Postsecondary Training

State requirements for school nurses vary. Some states have a certification requirement. Others require that their school nurses have bachelor's degrees while some do not require a bachelor's degree but do have specific educational requirements. There are some states that require their school nurses to be registered nurses. (See *Registered Nurses*.)

There is no special program for school nursing in basic RN education; however, most nursing programs have courses geared to the specialty such as health education, child or adolescent psychology, crisis intervention, community health, and growth and development.

Certification or Licensing

National certification is available through the National Board for Certification of School Nurses. Currently North Carolina and Massachusetts require national certification. Some states have state certification programs for school nurses.

In addition, some state education agencies set additional requirements such as nursing experience and competency in specified areas of health and education. Local or regional boards of education may also have certain qualifications that they require of their school nurses.

Other Requirements

School nurses must have patience and like working with children and teens. They must also be able to work well with teachers, parents, administrators, and other health personnel. School nurses should be able to work independently since they often work alone.

Exploring

You can explore your interest in the nursing field in a number of ways. You can read books on careers in nursing and talk with high school guidance counselors, school nurses, and local public health nurses. Visit hospitals to observe the work and to talk with hospital personnel.

Some hospitals now have extensive volunteer service programs in which students can work after school, on weekends, or during vacations. You can find other volunteer work experiences with the Red Cross or community health services. Camp counseling jobs sometimes offer related experiences. Some schools offer participation in Future Nurses programs.

Employers

Nurses are employed by hospitals, managed-care facilities, long-term-care facilities, clinics, industry, private homes, schools, camps, and government agencies.

Starting Out

The only way to become a registered nurse is through completion of one of the three kinds of educational programs, plus passing the licensing examination. Registered nurses may apply for employment directly to hospitals, nursing homes, companies, and government agencies that hire nurses. Jobs can also be obtained through school placement offices, by signing up with employment agencies specializing in placement of nursing personnel, or through the state employment office. Other sources of jobs include nurses' associations, professional journals, and newspaper want ads.

Advancement

Administrative and supervisory positions in the nursing field go to nurses who have earned at least the bachelor of science degree in nursing. Nurses with many years of experience who are graduates of the diploma program may achieve supervisory positions, but requirements for such promotions have become more difficult in recent years and in many cases require at least the bachelor of science in nursing degree.

Earnings

According to the U.S. Department of Labor's *Occupational Outlook Handbook,* registered nurses earned an average of $40,690 annually in 1998. The low 10 percent earned less than $29,480, while the middle 50 percent earned between $34,430 and $49,070. The top 10 percent made over $69,300 a year. However, school nurses' salaries may differ.

School nurses' salaries are determined by several factors—the financial status of the school district, the nurse's experience, and the scope of duties. According to a 1996 survey by the Health Resources and Services Administration at the U.S. Department of Health and Human Services, full-time registered school nurses earned about $32,000.

Work Environment

Schools are found in all communities, cities, and rural areas, and learning institutions can vary greatly. School nurses may work in an environment that is a state-of-the-art educational institution in an affluent community, or they may work in a rundown building in the inner city. By the same token, some school nurses may have up-to-date equipment and adequate resources, while others may find that they have restricted funds that inhibit their ability to do their jobs.

School nurses usually work days and may have some time off during the summer months when school is not in session.

The increase in school violence impacts the school nurses' working environment since it is evident that acts of violence can occur in any institution in any community. School nurses must be prepared to deal with the physical results of violence in their schools.

School nurses may come in contact with infectious diseases and are often exposed to illnesses and injuries. All nursing careers have some health and disease risks; however, adherence to health and safety guidelines greatly minimizes the chance of contracting infectious diseases such as hepatitis and AIDS.

Outlook

Nursing specialties will be in great demand in the future. The U.S. Bureau of Labor Statistics lists nursing as one of 10 occupations with the largest growth rate. From 1998 to 2008, jobs in nursing are expected to increase by 21.6 percent. Employment for registered nurses, according to the U.S. Bureau of Labor Statistics, projects that employment for registered nurses will grow faster than the average for all occupations through 2008.

However, according to the National Association of School Nurses, even though school enrollments are projected to increase, school nurse positions are being eliminated in a greater proportion than other positions within the educational system. As educational systems try to find ways to cut costs, professionals such as school nurses may be eliminated. Since cuts may vary by region and state, school nurses should be flexible and willing to relocate or to seek other nursing opportunities, if necessary.

For More Information

American Association of Colleges of Nursing
One Dupont Circle, NW, Suite 530
Washington, DC 20036
Tel: 202-463-6930
Web: http://www.aacn.nche.edu

National Association of School Nurses
PO Box 1300
Scarborough, ME 04070-1300
Tel: 207-883-2117
Web: http://www.nasn.org

Transplant Coordinators

	School Subjects
Biology	
Chemistry	

	Personal Interests
Helping/teaching	
Technical/scientific	

	Work Environment
Primarily indoors	
Primarily multiple locations	

	Minimum Education Level
Bachelor's degree	

	Salary Range
$30,000 to $50,000 to $70,000	

	Certification or Licensing
Voluntary	

	Outlook
Faster than the average	

Overview

Transplantation (the act of transplanting organs and tissues) is a rapidly growing specialty in modern medicine. As transplantation has developed, the new health care specialty of *transplant coordinator* has evolved. These professionals possess specific knowledge in the areas of organ and tissue procurement and transplantation.

A transplant coordinator is involved in practically every aspect of organ procurement (getting the organ from the donor) and transplantation; this involves working with medical records, educating and procuring donors, scheduling surgeries, educating potential organ recipients, counseling donor families, and conducting follow-up research.

History

In 1954, the first successful human kidney transplant was performed in Boston. The 1960s brought many successes in the field of organ transplants including successful human liver and pancreas transplants. The first heart transplant was performed in 1967.

Despite these successes, many transplants eventually failed because of the body's immune system, which eventually rejected the new organ as a foreign object. Although drugs were designed in the 1960s to help the body accept transplanted organs, it wasn't until the early 1980s that a truly effective immunosuppressant drug, cyclosoporin, was available. This drug substantially improved the success rate of transplant surgeries. More precise tissue typing or matching of donor and recipient tissues also helped increase the success rate.

Though successful organ transplants have increased, some transplants still fail over time despite modern drug treatments and closer tissue matching. Research in this area continues with the hope of increasing the rate of successful transplants.

The Job

The vision of transplant coordinators, according to the National Association of Transplant Coordinators, is, "That there be a better quality of life for people with end stage organ and tissue failure . . . and a respect for those who shared."

A transplant coordinator acts as a liaison between the patient, family, and physician. There are two types of transplant coordinators—*procurement coordinators* and *clinical coordinators*.

Most procurement coordinators work for a tissue or organ procurement organization (OPO), which is an independent agency that serves as a link between transplant centers and hospitals. Procurement coordinators maintain the viability of donor's organs until they can be transplanted. This includes ordering tests after the patient is determined brain dead to determine if the organs can be transplanted. The procurement coordinator then searches for a recipient/donor match, calls the recipient's physician to offer them the organ, and then contacts the necessary surgeons to remove the donated organs. Next, the procurement coordinator is in charge of overseeing what takes place in the operating room and acts as a liaison between the donor's family and the organ recipient, making sure everything is done ethically, and arranging for optimal organ care and transportation.

One of the main responsibilities of the procurement coordinator is helping the families of an organ donor deal with the death of a loved one as well as informing them about the organ donation process. Julie Petro, a procurement coordinator in Philadelphia, emphasizes the importance of counseling families of organ donors. "People don't understand how much of this job has to do with the families. Half of our training is in bereavement issues. We're trying to help families, too, not just trying to help people get organs." This may involve keeping in touch with the donor family long after the death of the organ donor to answer any questions the family may have. Although actual organ recipients' names aren't given to donor families, some families like to be updated as to the recipients' health and progress.

Because of the urgency of the transplantation process, procurement coordinators are almost always on call and may work long, irregular hours. Sometimes they may put in as many as 70 hours a week. Procurement coordinators might need to fly to another state to get an organ from an OPO for a patient in their area.

Clinical coordinators also work for organ procurement agencies. They educate recipients so they can be prepared for their organ transplant and address any concerns they may have while waiting for their surgery. They also educate patients and their families on various treatment options. After receiving the transplant, clinical coordinators monitor patients' conditions and keep other members of the transplant team informed of their progress. The clinical coordinators help patients have smooth and successful recoveries and begin their return to normal lives. Former patients are kept up-to-date on new and more effective therapies for managing their health through the clinical coordinator.

Both procurement and clinical coordinators are involved in presenting informational and educational programs to hospitals, nursing staffs, communities, and organizations regarding the need for organ and tissue donors.

Requirements

Postsecondary Training

Bachelor's or advanced degrees may be required for coordinator positions. Many facilities, agencies, and organizations require that their transplant coordinators be registered nurses. (See *Registered Nurses*.) Some transplant coordinators have degrees in biology, physiology, accounting, psychology, business administration, or public health. Medical, business, and social work experience are valuable for this position.

Certification or Licensing

Certification as a procurement transplant coordinator and a clinical transplant coordinator are available through the American Board of Transplant Coordinators and may be a requirement for some jobs.

Other Requirements

Transplant coordinators must be detail-oriented, have excellent organizational skills, and be able to make intelligent decisions. They must also be assertive and demand that procedures are done correctly and expediently. Because coordinators work with families suffering the loss of a loved one, or with sick patients needing an organ transplant, they must be caring and compassionate. A transplant coordinator also needs to be prepared to deal with death on a daily basis.

Employers

A number of different institutions and organizations require transplant coordinators. In addition to the 281 transplant centers across the country, there are 56 independent organ procurement organizations and 56 independent tissue-typing labs. There are also 12 organ procurement organizations and 100 tissue-typing labs within the transplant centers themselves. These organizations and centers may be hospital-based, independent, or university-based.

Starting Out

Positions for transplant coordinators are advertised nationally in medical publications and on the Internet. The North American Transplant Coordinators Organization (NATCO) also offers job referral information.

Many transplant coordinators begin their professional careers in other areas such as nursing, business, psychology, social work, or the sciences before they seek a career as a transplant coordinator.

Advancement

There may be internal advancement opportunities within a clinic such as senior coordinator or senior educator. Other managerial or supervisory positions may also be a way of advancing within the career. There are other aspects of transplantation, such as surgery or hospital administration, that may be available with additional education and experience.

Earnings

Educational background, experience, responsibilities, and geographic location determine earnings as a coordinator.

The salary range for transplant coordinators is about the same as registered nurses. According to the U.S. Department of Labor's *Occupational Outlook Handbook,* registered nurses earned an average of $40,690 annually in 1998. The low 10 percent earned less than $29,480, while the middle 50 percent earned between $34,430 and $49,070. The top 10 percent made over $69,300 a year. Transplant coordinators in certain areas may earn more. Coordinators who are in administrative and supervisory positions, and those with advanced degrees, can expect to make more.

Employers usually provide health and life insurance, and some offer educational reimbursements.

Work Environment

Nearly all transplant coordinators work for an independent organ or tissue procurement agency. Most transplant centers are located in larger populated areas and serve a greater geographic region. Procurement coordinators can expect to travel to other locations at a moment's notice. Clinical and procurement coordinators must travel to transplant centers or hospitals at all hours of the day and night so personal safety may be an issue in some areas.

All health-related careers have some health and disease risks; however, adherence to health and safety guidelines greatly minimizes the chance of contracting infectious diseases such as hepatitis and AIDS. Medical knowledge and good safety measures are also needed to limit the coordinator's exposure to toxic chemicals, radiation, and other hazards.

Outlook

The need for organ donors continues to grow, which will create an increased demand for transplant coordinators. Although the number of organ donors is increasing, the need continues to exceed the supply. In April 2000, the United Network for Organ Sharing (UNOS) reported that over 69,000 people were waiting for some type of organ transplant.

There is a large turnover in this career field creating ongoing job opportunities as well. Job burnout often occurs in this profession because transplant coordinators frequently work long, irregular hours. In addition, the emotional demands of the job can often take a toll on these professionals. However, coordinators who have nursing backgrounds and choose to get out of the transplant coordinator field should find good career opportunities in health-related fields.

For More Information

International Transplant Nurses Society
1739 E. Carson Street, Box #351
Pittsburgh, PA 15203-1700
Tel: 412-488-0240
Web: http://www.itns.org/

North American Transplant Coordinators Organization
PO Box 15384
Lenexa, KS 66285-5384
Tel: 913-492-3600
Web: http://www.natco1.org

United Network for Organ Sharing
1100 Boulders Parkway, Suite 500
PO Box 13770
Richmond, VA 23225-8770
Tel: 804-330-8500
Web: http://www.unos.org

This Web site is an excellent educational resource regarding organ donations and transplants.

Web: http://www.transweb.org

For information on certification, contact:

American Board of Transplant Coordinators
8310 Nieman Road
Lenexa, KS 66214
Tel: 913-599-0198

State Boards of Nursing

Alabama Board of Nursing
RSA Plaza, Suite 250
770 Washington Avenue
Montgomery, AL 36130-3900
Tel: 334-242-4060
Fax: 334-242-4360

Alaska Board of Nursing
Department of Commerce and Economic Development
Division of Occupational Licensing
3601 C Street, Suite 722
Anchorage, AK 99503
Tel: 907-269-8161
Fax: 907-269-8196

American Samoa Health Services
Regulatory Board
LBJ Tropical Medical Center
Pago Pago, AS 96799
Tel: 684-633-1222
Fax: 684-633-1869

Arizona State Board of Nursing
1651 E. Morten Avenue, Suite 150
Phoenix, AZ 85020
Tel: 602-331-8111
Fax: 602-906-9365

Arkansas State Board of Nursing
University Tower Building
1123 South University, Suite 800
Little Rock, AR 72204
Tel: 501-686-2700
Fax: 501-686-2714

California Board of Registered Nursing
400 R Street, Suite 4030
Sacramento, CA 95814-6239
Tel: 916-322-3350
Fax: 916-327-4402

California Board of Vocational Nurse and Psychiatric Technician Examiners
2535 Capitol Oaks Drive, Suite 205
Sacramento, CA 95833
Tel: 916-263-7800
Fax: 916-263-7859

Colorado Board of Nursing
1560 Broadway, Suite 880
Denver, CO 80202
Tel: 303-894-2430
Fax: 303-894-2821

Commonwealth Board of Nurse Examiners
Public Health Center
PO Box 1458
Saipan, MP 96950
Tel: 670-234-8950
Fax: 670-234-8930

Commonwealth of Puerto Rico Board of Nurse Examiners
800 Roberto H. Todd Avenue
Room 202, Stop 18
Santurce, PR 00908
Tel: 787-725-8161
Fax: 787-725-7903

Connecticut Board of Examiners for Nursing
Division of Health Systems Regulation
410 Capitol Avenue, MS# 12HSR
PO Box 340308
Hartford, CT 06134-0328
Tel: 860-509-7624
Fax: 860-509-7553

Delaware Board of Nursing
861 Silver Lake Boulevard
Cannon Building, Suite 203
Dover, DE 19904
Tel: 302-739-4522
Fax: 302-739-2711

District of Columbia Board of Nursing
Department of Health
825 North Capitol Street, NE, 2nd Floor
Room 2224
Washington, DC 20002
Tel: 202-442-4778
Fax: 202-442-9431

Florida Board of Nursing
4080 Woodcock Drive, Suite 202
Jacksonville, FL 32207
Tel: 904-858-6940
Fax: 904-858-6964

Georgia State Board of Licensed Practical Nurses
237 Coliseum Drive
Macon, GA 31217-1640
Tel: 912-207-1300
Fax: 912-207-1363

Georgia Board of Nursing
237 Coliseum Drive
Macon, GA 31217-3858
Tel: 912-207-1640
Fax: 912-207-1660

Guam Board of Nurse Examiners
PO Box 2816
1304 East Sunset Boulevard
Barrgada, GU 96913
Tel: 671-475-0251
Fax: 671-477-4733

Hawaii Board of Nursing
Professional and Vocational Licensing Division
PO Box 3469
Honolulu, HI 96801
Tel: 808-586-3000
Fax: 808-586-2689

Idaho Board of Nursing
280 N. 8th Street, Suite 210
PO Box 83720
Boise, ID 83720
Tel: 208-334-3110
Fax: 208-334-3262

Illinois Department of Professional Regulation
James R. Thompson Center
100 West Randolph, Suite 9-300
Chicago, IL 60601
Tel: 312-814-2715
Fax: 312-814-3145

Indiana State Board of Nursing
Health Professions Bureau
402 West Washington Street, Room W041
Indianapolis, IN 46204
Tel: 317-232-2960
Fax: 317-233-4236

Iowa Board of Nursing
RiverPoint Business Park
400 SW 8th Street, Suite B
Des Moines, IA 50309-4685
Tel: 515-281-3255
Fax: 515-281-4825

Kansas State Board of Nursing
Landon State Office Building
900 SW Jackson, Suite 551-S
Topeka, KS 66612
Tel: 785-296-4929
Fax: 785-296-3929

Kentucky Board of Nursing
312 Whittington Parkway, Suite 300
Louisville, KY 40222
Tel: 502-329-7000
Fax: 502-329-7011

Louisiana State Board of Practical Nurse Examiners
3421 North Causeway Boulevard, Suite 203
Metairie, LA 70002
Tel: 504-838-5791
Fax: 504-838-5279

Louisiana State Board of Nursing
3510 North Causeway Boulevard, Suite 501
Metairie, LA 70003
Tel: 504-838-5332
Fax: 504-838-5349

Maine State Board of Nursing
158 State House Station
Augusta, ME 04333
Tel: 207-287-1133
Fax: 207-287-1149

Maryland Board of Nursing
4140 Patterson Avenue
Baltimore, MD 21215
Tel: 410-585-1900
Fax: 410-358-3530

Massachusetts Board of Registration in Nursing

Commonwealth of Massachusetts
239 Causeway Street
Boston, MA 02114
Tel: 617-727-9961
Fax: 617-727-1630

Michigan CIS/Office of Health Services

Ottawa Towers North
611 West Ottawa, 4th Floor
Lansing, MI 48933
Tel: 517-373-9102
Fax: 517-373-2179

Minnesota Board of Nursing

2829 University Avenue, SE, Suite 500
Minneapolis, MN 55414
Tel: 612-617-2270
Fax: 612-617-2190

Mississippi Board of Nursing

1935 Lakeland Drive, Suite B
Jackson, MS 39216
Tel: 601-987-4188
Fax: 601-364-2352

Missouri State Board of Nursing

3605 Missouri Boulevard
PO Box 656
Jefferson City, MO 65102-0656
Tel: 573-751-0681
Fax: 573-751-0075

Montana State Board of Nursing

Arcade Building, Suite 4C
111 North Jackson
Helena, MT 59620-0513
Tel: 406-444-2071
Fax: 406-444-7759

Nebraska Health and Human Services System

Department of Regulation and Licensure, Nursing Section
301 Centennial Mall South
PO Box 94986
Lincoln, NE 68509-4986
Tel: 402-471-4376
Fax: 402-471-3577

Nevada State Board of Nursing

1755 East Plumb Lane, Suite 260
Reno, NV 89502
Tel: 775-688-2620
Fax: 775-688-2628

New Hampshire Board of Nursing

78 Regional Drive, Building B
PO Box 3898
Concord, NH 03302
Tel: 603-271-2323
Fax: 603-271-6605

New Jersey Board of Nursing

124 Halsey Street, 6th Floor
PO Box 45010
Newark, NJ 07101
Tel: 973-504-6586
Fax: 973-648-3481

New Mexico Board of Nursing

4206 Louisiana Boulevard, NE, Suite A
Albuquerque, NM 87109
Tel: 505-841-8340
Fax: 505-841-8347

New York State Board of Nursing

State Education Department
Cultural Education Center, Room 3023
Albany, NY 12230
Tel: 518-474-3845
Fax: 518-474-3706

North Carolina Board of Nursing
 3724 National Drive, Suite 201
 Raleigh, NC 27612
 Tel: 919-782-3211
 Fax: 919-781-9461

North Dakota Board of Nursing
 919 South 7th Street, Suite 504
 Bismark, ND 58504
 Tel: 701-328-9777
 Fax: 701-328-9785

Ohio Board of Nursing
 17 South High Street, Suite 400
 Columbus, OH 43215-3413
 Tel: 614-466-3947
 Fax: 614-466-0388

Oklahoma Board of Nursing
 2915 North Classen Boulevard, Suite 524
 Oklahoma City, OK 73106
 Tel: 405-962-1800
 Fax: 405-962-1821

Oregon State Board of Nursing
 800 NE Oregon Street, Box 25, Suite 465
 Portland, OR 97232
 Tel: 503-731-4745
 Fax: 503-731-4755

Pennsylvania State Board of Nursing
 124 Pine Street
 PO Box 2649
 Harrisburg, PA 17101
 Tel: 717-783-7142
 Fax: 717-783-0822

Rhode Island Board of Nurses Registration and Nursing Education
Registration and Nursing Education
105 Cannon Building
Three Capitol Hill
Providence, RI 02908
Tel: 401-222-5700
Fax: 401-222-3352

South Carolina State Board of Nursing
110 Centerview Drive, Suite 202
Columbia, SC 29210
Tel: 803-896-4550
Fax: 803-896-4525

South Dakota Board of Nursing
4300 South Louise Avenue, Suite C-1
Sioux Falls, SD 57106-3124
Tel: 605-362-2760
Fax: 605-362-2768

Tennessee State Board of Nursing
426 Fifth Avenue North, 1st Floor
Cordell Hull Building
Nashville, TN 37247
Tel: 615-532-5166
Fax: 615-741-7899

Texas Board of Nurse Examiners
333 Guadalupe, Suite 3-460
Austin, TX 78701
Tel: 512-305-7400
Fax: 512-305-7401

Texas Board of Vocational Nurse Examiners
William P. Hobby Building, Tower 3
333 Guadalupe Street, Suite 3-400
Austin, TX 78701
Tel: 512-305-8100
Fax: 512-305-8101

Utah State Board of Nursing
Heber M. Wells Building, 4th Floor
160 East 300 South
Salt Lake City, UT 84111
Tel: 801-530-6628
Fax: 801-530-6511

Vermont State Board of Nursing
109 State Street
Montpelier, VT 05609-1106
Tel: 802-828-2396
Fax: 802-828-2484

Virgin Islands Board of Nurse Licensure
Veterans Drive Station
St. Thomas, VI 00803
Tel: 340-776-7397
Fax: 340-777-4003

Virginia Board of Nursing
6606 West Broad Street, 4th Floor
Richmond, VA 23230
Tel: 804-662-9909
Fax: 804-662-9512

Washington State Nursing Care Quality
Assurance Commission
Department of Health
1300 Quince Street, SE
Olympia, WA 98504-7864
Tel: 360-236-4740
Fax: 360-236-4738

West Virginia State Board of Examiners for Licensed Practical Nurses
101 Dee Drive
Charleston, WV 25311
Tel: 304-558-3572
Fax: 304-558-4367

West Virginia Board of Examiners for Registered Professional Nurses

101 Dee Drive
Charleston, WV 25311
Tel: 304-558-3596
Fax: 304-558-3666

Wisconsin Department of Regulation and Licensing

1400 East Washington Avenue
PO Box 8935
Madison, WI 53708
Tel: 608-266-2112
Fax: 608-267-0644

Wyoming State Board of Nursing

2020 Carey Avenue, Suite 110
Cheyenne, WY 82002
Tel: 307-777-7601
Fax: 307-777-3519

Nursing Organizations

American Academy of Ambulatory Care Nurses
East Holly Avenue, Box 56
Pitman, NJ 08071
Tel: 609-256-2350
Fax: 609-589-7463
Email: aaacn@mail.ajj.com
Web: http://aaacn.inurse.com/

American Academy of Medical-Surgical Nurses
AMSN National Office
East Holly Avenue, Box 56
Pitman, NJ 08071-0056
Tel: 856-256-2323
Fax: 856-589-7463
Email: amsn@ajj.com
Web: http://www.medsurgnurse.org/

American Academy of Nurse Practitioners
Capital Station
PO Box 12846
Austin, TX 78711
Tel: 512-442-4262
Fax: 512-442-6469
Email: admin@aanp.org
Web: http://www.aanp.org/

American Academy of Nursing
600 Maryland Avenue, Suite 100 West
Washington, DC 20024-2571
Tel: 202-651-7238
Fax: 202-554-2641
Web: http://www.nursingworld.org/aan

American Assembly for Men in Nursing
NYSNA
11 Cornell Road
Latham, NY 12110
Tel: 518-782-9400, ext. 346
Fax: 518-782-9530
Email: aamn@nysna.org
Web: http://www.aamn.org/

American Association for the History of Nursing
PO Box 175
Lanoka Harbor, NJ 08734
Tel: 609-693-7250
Fax: 609-693-1037
Email: AAHN@aahn.org
Web: http://www.aahn.org/aahn.html

American Association of Critical-Care Nurses
101 Columbia
Aliso Viejo, CA 92656
Tel: 714-362-2000
Fax: 714-362-2020
Email: aacninfo@aacn.org
Web: http://www.aacn.org/

American Association of Legal Nurse Consultants
4700 West Lake Ave.
Glenview, IL 60025
Tel: 847-375-4713
Fax: 847-375-4777
Email: info@aalnc.org
Web: http://www.aalnc.org/

American Association of Neuroscience Nurses
224 Des Plaines, No. 601
Chicago, IL 60661
Tel: 312-993-0043
Fax: 312-993-0362
Email: assnneuro@aol.com
Web: http://www.aann.org/

American Association of Nurse Anesthetists

222 South Prospect Avenue
Park Ridge, IL 60068-4001
Tel: 708-692-7050
Fax: 708-692-6968

American Association of Nurse Attorneys

7794 Grow Drive
Pensacola, FL 32514-7072
Tel: 850-474-3646
Fax: 850-484-8762
Email: TAANA@puetzamc.com
Web: http://www.taana.org/

American Association of Occupational Health Nurses

2920 Brandywine Road
Atlanta, GA 30341
Tel: 770-455-7757
Fax: 770-455-7271
Web: http://www.aaohn.org/

American Association of Spinal Cord Injury Nurses

75-20 Astoria Boulevard
Jackson Heights, NY 11370-1177
Tel: 718-803-3782
Fax: 718-803-0414
Web: http://www.aascin.org/

American College of Nurse Practitioners

503 Capitol Court, NE, Suite 300
Washington, DC 20002
Fax: 202-546-4797
Tel: 202-546-4825
Email: acnp@nurse.org
Web: http://www.nurse.org/acnp

American College of Nurse-Midwives

818 Connecticut Avenue, NW, Suite 900
Washington, DC 20006
Tel: 202-728-9860
Fax: 202-728-9897
Email: info@acnm.org
Web: http://www.midwife.org/

American Forensic Nurses

255 N. El Cielo, Suite 195
Palm Springs, CA 92262
Web: http://www.amrn.com/

American Holistic Nurses Association

PO Box 2130
Flagstaff, AZ 86003-2130

American Licensed Practical Nurses Association

1090 Vermont Ave, NW, Suite 1200
Washington, DC 20005
Tel: 202-682-5800
Fax: 202-682-0168

American Nephrology Nurses Association

East Holly Avenue, Box 56
Pitman, NJ 08071-0056
Tel: 609-256-2320
Fax: 609-589-7463
Email: anna@mail.com
Web: http://anna.inurse.com/

American Nurses Association

600 Maryland Avenue, SW, Suite 100 West
Washington, DC 20024-2571
Tel: 202-651-7012
Fax: 202-651-7001
Email: main@ana.org
Web: http://www.nursingworld.org/

American Nursing Assistants Association
PO Box 15
Lena, IL 61048-0015

American Psychiatric Nurses Association
1200 19th Street, NW, Suite 300
Washington, DC 20036-2422
Tel: 202-857-1133
Fax: 202-857-1102
Email: apna@dc.sba.com
Web: http://www.apna.org/

American Radiological Nurses Association
2021 Spring Road, Suite 600
Oak Brook, IL 60523
Tel: 630-571-9072
Fax: 630-571-7837
Email: arna@rsna.org

American Society of Ophthalmic Registered Nurses
PO Box 193030
San Francisco, CA 94119
Tel: 415-561-8513
Fax: 415-561-8575
Email: asorn@aao.org

American Society of Pain Management Nurses
7794 Grow Drive
Pensacola, FL 32514-7072
Tel: 850-473-0233
Fax: 850-484-8762
Email: ASPMN@puetzamc.com

American Society of Plastic and Reconstructive Surgical Nurses
East Holly Avenue
Pitman, NJ 08071
Tel: 609-256-2340
Fax: 609-589-7463
Email: asprsn@mail.ajj.com
Web: http://www.asprsn.inurse.com/

Association of Rehabilitation Nurses
4700 West Lake Road
Glenview, IL 60025-1485
Tel: 708-966-3433
Fax: 708-375-4700

Association of Women's Health, Obstetric and Neonatal Nursing
2000 L Street, NW, Suite 740
Washington, DC 20036
Tel: 202-261-2400
Fax: 202-728-0575
Email: annef@awhonn.org
Web: http://www.awhonn.org/

Dermatology Nurses Association
Box 56
North Woodbury Road
Pitman, NJ 08071
Fax: 609-582-1915

Developmental Disabilities Nurses Association
1720 Willow Creek Circle, Suite 515
Eugene, OR 97402
Tel: 800-888-6733
Fax: 541-485-7372

Emergency Nurses Association
915 Lee Street
Des Plaines, IL 60016-6569
Tel: 800-900-9659
Fax: 847-460-4001
Email: enainfo@ena.org
Web: http://www.ena.org/

Home Health Care Nurses Association
228 7th Street, SE
Washington, DC 20003
Tel: 1-800-558-HHNA
Fax: 202-547-3540
Email: HHNA@puetzamc.com

Association of Black Nursing Faculty, Inc.

1708 North Roxboro Road
Durham, NC 20009

Association of Community Health Nursing Educators

7794 Grow Drive
Pensacola, FL 32514-7072
Tel: 850-474-8821
Fax: 850-484-8762
Email: ACHNE@puetzamc.com

Association of Nurses Endorsing Transplantation

PO Box 5412
Merrit Island, FL 32954-1234
Tel: 407-459-3777
Email: aidsnurses@aol.com

Association of Nurses in AIDS Care

11250 Roger Bacon Drive, Suite 8
Reston, VA 20190
Tel: 202-462-1038
Web: http://www.anacnet.org/

Association of Operating Room Nurses

2170 South Parker Road, Suite 300
Denver, CO 80231-5711
Tel: 303-755-6304
Fax: 303-750-2927
Web: http://www.aorn.org/

Association of Pediatric Oncology Nurses

4700 West Lake Avenue
Glenview, IL 60025-1485
Tel: 708-966-3723
Fax: 708-375-4777

National Association of Orthopedic Nurses
Box 56
East Holly Avenue
Pitman, NJ 08071-0056
Tel: 609-256-2310
Fax: 609-589-7463
Email: naon@mail.ajj.com
Web: http://naon.inurse.com/

National Association of Pediatric Nurse Associates and Practitioners
1101 Kings Highway North, Suite 206
Cherry Hill, NJ 08034
Tel: 609-667-1773
Fax: 609-667-7187
Email: napnap1@aol.com
Web: http://www.napnap.org/

National Association of Registered Nurses
11508 Allecingie Parkway, Suite C
Richmond, VA 23235
Tel: 804-794-6513
Fax: 804-379-7698

National Association of School Nurses
PO Box 1300
Scarborough, ME 04070-1300
Tel: 207-883-2117
Fax: 207-883-2683
Email: nasn@aol.com
Web: http://www.nasn.org/

National Black Nurses Association, Inc.
1511 K Street, NW, Suite 415
Washington, DC 20005
Tel: 202-393-6870
Fax: 202-347-3808
Email: nbna@erols.com

Hospice Nurses Association
5512 North Umberland Street
Pittsburgh, PA 15217-1131
Tel: 412-687-3231
Fax: 412-687-9095

Indian American Nurses Association
270 First Avenue, Suite 3D
New York, NY 10009

National Association for Practical Nurse Education and Service
1400 Spring Street, Suite 330
Silver Spring, MD 20910
Tel: 301-588-2491
Fax: 301-588-2839
Email: napnes@bellatlantic.net

National Association of Hispanic Nurses
1501 16th Street, NW
Washington, DC 20036
Tel: 202-387-2477
Fax: 202-483-7183
Email: nahn.juno.com
Web: http://www.nahnhq.org/

National Association of Neonatal Nurses
701 Lee Street, Suite 450
Des Plaines, IL 60016
Tel: 800-451-3795
Tel: 847-299-6266
Fax: 847-297-6768
Email: info@nann.org
Web: http://www.nann.org/

National Association of Nurse Practitioners in Reproductive Health
2401 Pennsylvania Avenue, NW
Washington, DC 20037
Tel: 202-466-4825
Fax: 202-466-3826

National Council of State Boards of Nursing, Inc.
676 North St. Clair, Suite 550
Chicago, IL 60611-2921
Tel: 312-787-6555
Fax: 312-787-6898
Web: http://www.ncsbn.org/

National Federation of Licensed Practical Nurses, Inc.
1418 Aversboro Road
Garner, NC 27529
Tel: 919-779-0046
Fax: 919-779-5642
Web: http://www.nflpn.com/

National Flight Nurses Association
6900 Grove Road
Thorofare, NJ 08086

National Gerontological Nursing Association
7794 Grow Drive
Pensacola, FL 32514-7072
Tel: 850-473-1174
Fax: 580-484-8762
Email: NGNA@puetzamc.com
Web: http://www.nursingcenter.com/people/nrsorgs/ngna/

National League for Nursing
61 Broadway, 33rd Floor
New York, NY 10006
Tel: 212-363-5555
Fax: 212-812-0393
Web: http://www.nln.org/

National Organization for Associate Degree Nursing
11250 Roger Bacon Drive, Suite 8
Reston, VA 20190
Tel: 703-437-4377
Fax: 703-435-4390
Email: noadn@noadn.org
Web: http://www.noadn.org/

National Student Nurses Association

555 West 57th Street, Suite 1327
New York, NY 10019
Tel: 212-581-2211
Fax: 212-581-2368
Email: nsna@nsna.org
Web: http://www.nsna.org/

Nurses Educational Funds

555 West 57th Street, 13th Floor
New York, NY 10019
Tel: 212-582-8820 x806

Oncology Nursing Society

501 Holiday Drive
Pittsburgh, PA 15220-2749
Tel: 412-921-7373
Fax: 412-921-6565
Email: customer.service@ons.org
Web: http://www.ons.org/

Respiratory Nursing Society

7794 Grow Drive
Pensacola, FL 32514-7072
Tel: 850-474-8869
Fax: 850-484-8762
Email: RNS@puetzamc.com

Society for Vascular Nursing

7794 Grow Drive
Pensacola, FL 32514-7072
Tel: 850-474-6963
Fax: 850-484-8762
Email: SVN@puetzamc.com

Society of Gastroenterology Nurses and Associates
401 North Michigan Avenue
Chicago, IL 60611
Tel: 800-245-7462
Fax: 312-321-5194
Email: sgna@sba.com
Web: http://www.sgna.org/

Society of Trauma Nurses
1211 Locust Street
Philadelphia, PA 19107
Tel: 800-237-6966
Fax: 215-545-8107

Visiting Nurse Associations of America
3801 East Florida, Suite 900
Denver, CO 80210
Tel: 303-753-0248
Fax: 303-753-0258

Wound Ostomy and Continence Nurses
2755 Bristol Street, Suite 110
Costa Mesa, CA 92626
Tel: 714-476-0268
Fax: 714-545-3643

Abbreviations

ACNM	American College of Nurse-Midwives
ANA	American Nurses Association
APN	Advanced Practice Nurse
BSN	Bachelor of Science in Nursing
CNA	Certified Nursing Assistant
CNM	Certified Nurse-Midwife
CNS	Certified Nurse Specialist
CPM	Certified Professional Midwife
CRNA	Certified Registered Nurse Anesthetist
ER	Emergency Room
FNP	Family Nurse Practitioner
HMO	Health Maintenance Organization
LNCC	Legal Nurse Consultant Certified
LPN	Licensed Practical Nurse
NARM	North American Registry of Midwives
NLN	National League of Nursing
NP	Nurse Practitioner
PA	Physician Assistant
PND	Pediatric Nurse Practitioner
RN	Registered Nurse

Index